Jamila Gavin

THE
SINGING BOWLS

Teens · Mandarin

First published in Great Britain 1989
by Methuen Children's Books Ltd
Published 1990 by Teens · Mandarin
an imprint of Mandarin Paperbacks
Michelin House, 81 Fulham Road, London SW3 6RB

Mandarin is an imprint of the Octopus Publishing Group

Copyright © 1989 Jamila Gavin

ISBN 0 7497 0332 6

A CIP catalogue record for this title
is available from the British Library

Printed in Great Britain
by Cox & Wyman Ltd, Reading, Berkshire

It all started in India . . .

Ronnie knew that his 'grandfather' had adopted his father as a baby in India, brought him to England and called him Adam. It hadn't meant much to Ronnie – the knowledge that he was half Indian. Like his father, he'd been brought up to feel completely English in thought, word and deed. His Indian blood had been deemed at best, exotic, and at worst something best not talked about, especially after his father had mysteriously disappeared.

'Now my beloved old grandfather is dying and the last link with my father dies, too, and the answers to all my unasked questions. I want to know about my father. No one tells me anything. I don't even know anything about India and I'm half Indian. Oh, I don't mean all that Empire stuff – I mean the real India. The India of the Indians. My father's India. Who was my father? Who was my grandfather – my real one, I mean. What other family have I got in India? Why is everyone so mysterious about it?'

And so Ronnie begins his quest that takes him eventually to the India of today when Ronnie goes with the singing bowls his father has left him as his only legacy, to try and find him there.

*Also by Jamila Gavin
for younger readers*

THREE INDIAN PRINCESSES
THE MAGIC ORANGE TREE
KAMLA AND KATE
ALI AND THE ROBOT
THE HIDEAWAY

Contents

1

BEFORE IT'S TOO LATE

'Are you there, Ronnie?'

'Yes, Grandpa.' Ronnie's silhouette stirred in the bay window.

'You haven't been doing your homework without light again, have you?' The old voice berated him from across the room. 'Put the light on, boy!'

'It's OK, Grandpa. There's still plenty of light from outside. Besides, I didn't want to wake you.' Ronnie got up from the table where for the last two hours he had crouched over his books. He stretched, nearly six foot now, tall enough for his fingers to brush the ceiling, and then walked gently over to the bed in the far corner where his grandfather lay.

He looked down at the amazingly slight shape beneath the blankets, and the old, gnarled, bony hands which lay clasped under his chin. He reminded Ronnie of one of those marble effigies he had seen reclining on tombs in cathedrals.

'What subject tonight?' The old man asked. He looked up at his grandson with wide, alert blue eyes which belied the truth that his body was now quite worn out, and could not sustain life much longer.

'History. The Decline of the British Empire. Discuss,' sighed Ronnie. 'Oh, I'm never going to get my GCSE's! Well, I don't care. There won't be any jobs left by the time I leave school anyway, so why kill myself over it? Besides, I can always be a bricklayer or something,' he muttered vehemently.

'Oh Ronnie, Ronnie,' murmured the old man. 'If only I could help you.' He stretched out a hand, but the boy had already moved away and was standing in the bay window.

Ronnie knew his grandfather was dying, and he had no idea how he was going to bear it.

'Where's your mother?'

'She's at her evening class. Pottery, or something.' He shrugged indifferently.

'I thought she went to upholstery.'

'That's on Thursdays. Tuesday's pottery, Wednesday's keep fit. She does something nearly every evening. She can't stick being at home.' The words hung bitterly in the fading light.

'She's been lonely all these years since your father left home,' explained the old man softly. 'She's still young, you know, Ronnie.'

'So am I!' retorted Ronnie fiercely. 'But with her being out all the time, I'm stuck here – ' he stopped short and a sob broke up his voice.

'It's all right, Ronnie. I know what you're saying. I'd really be fine on my own, you know. You don't have to listen to the nurse. I don't need supervision day in day out like a baby.'

'Oh, Grandpa. It's not you. You're the only person worth talking to anyway. It's not that . . . it's . . .' He couldn't say it. The loneliness. The fear.

'I know, Ronnie, old chap.' His grandfather's voice pleaded with him. 'We understand each other, you and I. We always have. Come here.' He patted the side of the bed. 'Tell me what you know about the Decline of the British Empire. Surely I can help. After all, I was part of it . . .' his voice grew fainter . . . 'It all started in India . . .' His voice faded until the only sound was his shallow, rattly breathing as he drifted into sleep.

Ronnie stood motionless, still staring out of the window. The sodium street lamps glowed more orange as twilight deepened into an autumn evening. 'It's not as though we even share the same flesh and blood,' thought Ronnie, and suddenly the grey pavements outside, and the people hurrying home from work looked alien though he had watched from that window all his life. He knew that the old man had adopted his father as a baby in India, brought him to England and called him Adam. It hadn't meant much to Ronnie – the knowledge that he was half Indian. Like his father, he had been brought up to feel completely English in thought, word and deed. His Indian blood had been deemed at best, exotic, explaining his olive skin, straight black hair and dark brooding eyes, and at worst something best not talked about. Especially after his father mysteriously disappeared.

He had a distant but clearly focused memory of that day ten years ago. His father had left for work as usual; caught the same bus to the station; boarded the same train, the 8.05 to Victoria, and had never been seen again. He didn't turn up at the bank where he worked, and no one came forward to say he had been seen anywhere else. It was as though he had vanished into thin air.

The police were called in, of course, but what could they do? 'People vanish every day,' they said. 'It's not a crime to disappear if you're an adult. If he's dead, then his body will turn up. Nine times out of ten they do. Did he have any other relationships . . .?'

Ronnie could remember the tears, anguish and anger at all the questions. Worse than the police were the relatives – so called. His mother's family. 'I always said it was a mistake for our Linda to marry him,' he overheard one say to another. 'Mixed marriages never work. She's best off without him. Pity they had a child. It's the kid I feel sorry for, poor little devil.'

'If only his body would turn up,' wept his mother. 'At least it would put a stop to this hideous gossip.'

But a body did not turn up. A year later, almost to the day, a letter arrived from India. A thin, cheap, battered envelope, so

9

covered with stamps and Post Office franking that the address was barely legible. Ronnie never knew what was in the letter, but his father's name had never been mentioned again.

His mother, Linda, struggled for a while, trying to keep up the mortgage payments on their little terraced house. But in the end it was too much for her, and they moved in with his adopted grandfather.

'After all, my dear,' Ronnie remembered Grandpa saying, 'in a way I feel I brought all this trouble on you. I tried to bring him up as my own flesh and blood. We both did, Isabella and I. I don't know what went wrong or where we went wrong. Thank God Isabella is dead and doesn't have to bear this grief.'

The images and words came echoing into his mind as Ronnie tried to control his emotions. He tiptoed softly over to the bed and once more looked down on the old man. One hand still patted the side of the bed where he wanted Ronnie to sit. His jaw had dropped open in his sleep, and his yellow skin shrank into the hollows of his cheekbones and tightened across his upturned brow.

'This is how he will look when he is dead,' thought Ronnie. A rush of panic overwhelmed him. 'When this old man dies, the last link with my father dies, too, and the answers to all my unasked questions.' He dropped to his knees and desperately shook the old, thin hand.

The old man jerked. He shut his mouth and slapped his lips to wet them. 'Er . . . where was I now? Was I telling you about Mahatma Gandhi? I met him once, you know.' His eyes gazed up at Ronnie, blue and shining with recall.

'I want to know about my father,' cried Ronnie, still clasping the old man's hand. 'No one tells me anything. I don't even know anything about India and I'm half Indian! Oh I don't mean all that Empire stuff – I mean the real India. The India of the Indians. My father's India. Who was my father? Who was my grandfather – my real one, I mean. What other family have

10

I got in India? Why is everyone so mysterious about it – are they ashamed?'

The old man's eyes closed wearily. 'I should have told you a long time ago.' His voice faltered and grew faint. 'Now it's too late. I'm too tired. We thought it was for the best . . . We didn't want to bother your young head with it . . .'

Ronnie shook his hand again, urgently. 'But, Grandpa, you must tell me. I've got to know who I am. If I'm half Indian why don't I feel anything? Half of myself is a stranger to me, don't you see?'

There was a sudden silence. Ronnie dropped his grandfather's hand with terror. Was he dead? Had he killed him by trying to force him to answer his questions? He couldn't hear him breathing.

'Grandpa?' he whispered, hoarsely.

The blue eyes flew open. His voice spoke, suddenly firm and determined. 'I have something for you. It will answer most of your questions. I wrote in my will that you were to be given this when you were twenty-one but I realise now I was being stupid and old-fashioned. Forgive me, Ronnie. Get it now. It's on top of the wardrobe. An old attaché case. Find it, find it quickly.' He struggled to sit up.

Ronnie pressed him back gently and straightened his pillow. 'Hush, Grandpa. Hush. Don't move. I'll find it.'

He stood on tiptoe and groped along the edge of the heavy, mahogany, Victorian wardrobe. His fingers probed along the rim, fumbling among old newspapers and magazines, stirring up clouds of dust which spilled into his eyes and throat, choking him.

'Have you got it yet?' the old man cried impatiently.

'Not yet. I'll need a chair to get to the very back.' He heaved over his chair from the bay window and climbed up. Now he reached over to the very back, thrusting aside paper bags and unidentified items, until suddenly, his fingers gripped a handle. 'Is this it?' he cried excitedly. He dragged it towards him, shutting his eyes from the dust that came swirling down. With both hands, he lifted it and lowered it till he hugged it to his chest. 'I think I've got it.' His voice brimmed with excitement.

The attaché case was heavy. He carried it over to the bed and showed it to the old man. 'Is this it?'

The grandfather looked at it long and silently. Feeble fingers trailed along its dusty face. 'Yes, yes. It's been my constant companion all my working life. My father gave it to me when I was appointed to my job in India. It's yours now, Ronnie. Make it your companion, too. Inside you will find much that should help you know about yourself as well as understand me. Read it now. Read it . . . I'm too old and tired to tell you . . .' As if relieved from a great burden, he closed his eyes and sank back into a deep sleep.

Swiftly Ronnie took the case over to the table. He swept aside his homework, and brushed off the dust with the edge of the curtain. Even in the semi-darkness Ronnie could see it was a handsome case. Its rich, brown leather had been polished and cared for over half a century. And there were his grandfather's initials embossed in gold flowing letters. H.R.S. – Henry Ronald Saville.

He dragged over an old, brass lampstand from the corner, and angling its tossing, fringed lampshade so that the light fell directly on to the table, Ronnie pulled the tassel. A deep, yellow circle of light fell upon the case. Ronnie glanced over to the bed. The room receded into the darkness and the old man did not stir. Turning back into the light, Ronnie gripped the worn, brass catches and opened the case.

2

MISSING, PRESUMED DEAD

It took Ronnie a while to sort out the bundles of papers and letters he found. He spread them all out on the table carefully, for some were so old and thin they were crumbling at the edges. There were faded yellow newspaper cuttings; letters from England with George V stamps; letters from India with George V as Emperor of India. Some were bound in velvet ribbon, some were held together with thin rubber bands. Carefully he untied them all and arranged them before him like some elaborate jigsaw puzzle. 'Where shall I start?' he asked out loud. Then his eye caught a headline on a newspaper cutting.

NORTH INDIA GAZETTE TUESDAY 20 SEPTEMBER 1927
Assistant District Commissioner Missing

It has now been confirmed that the Assistant District Commissioner of the Durgapur District in the United Province, Henry Ronald Saville, is missing and there must now be serious fears for his safety.

It was reported two weeks ago that Saville had caused alarm by apparently going "up country" unexpectedly, and despite the fact that his servant was away that night, he had not left any instructions for him or left any other member of his staff details of his whereabouts.

Saville was well known for his habit of riding out alone with just a rifle and a bedroll, but with the discovery of both these items in his room, any impulsive hunting excursion must be discounted.

13

In a report submitted to the Police and the India Office by Saville's superior, Mr James Richmond, he reveals that Saville was engaged in delicate and dangerous operations concerned with tracking down a band of dacoits who have been terrorising the district for some time.

He says: 'With dacoit activity taking on serious proportions in our area, we found it intolerable that any of His Majesty's subjects should live in fear of life and property. Mr Saville's avowed aim was to protect, reassure and befriend, particularly those inhabitants of remote, outlying villages. He believed that only with their confidence and co-operation could the dacoits be overcome.'

In an attempt to break through the wall of fear and silence, Saville had offered a reward of fifty rupees for any information leading to capture. This was backed by a guarantee of absolute secrecy for the bandits maintain their power over the villages by their ruthless reprisals.

It is against this background and after the most intense search, involving three hundred men and trackers, covering an area of forty miles in radius, that we must reluctantly come to the conclusion that Henry Saville may have been lured away and is being held against his will.

A reward of two hundred rupees has been offered for any information regarding his whereabouts – alive or dead.

Ronnie whistled with amazement. Quickly he unclipped the cutting from a small bundle of letters. The letters looked so private and vulnerable that Ronnie could hardly bring himself to slide out the thin, white sheets. But as he did, he realised that they had been kept in order, and that all he need do now was open them one by one and read.

LETTER TO MISS ISABELLA MAYNE
DURGAPUR 21 SEPTEMBER 1927

Dear Miss Mayne,

It is with the most sincere regret that I have to inform you that your fiancé, Mr Henry Saville, is missing and that there are considerable fears for his safety. I enclose a full report and details of the search operation which was mounted with the help of the garrison.

I can assure you that every effort has been made to gain information on his whereabouts but so far to no avail.

Henry Saville was a highly respected colleague and servant of the British Civil Service, who brought the highest ideals to his conduct and work. His disappearance has shocked and saddened us all, both English and native alike.

Any further news we receive will be despatched to you immediately. In the meantime, do not hesitate to get in touch if you have any queries on the matter.

Be assured, dear Miss Mayne, that we are all doing our best to solve this mystery.

I remain your obedient servant,

   James Richmond
      Commissioner.

LETTER TO MISS ISABELLA MAYNE
10 NOVEMBER 1927 LUCKNOW U.P.

Dear Miss Mayne,

This is to inform you that the India Office have regretfully come to the conclusion that Henry Ronald Saville, Assistant District Commissioner of the Durgapur District, United Province, must now be presumed dead.

Since his disappearance on 9 September there has been no clue to his fate.

After an intensive search, much consultation and deliberation, my officers and advisors have little doubt that Henry Saville was lured to his death, probably at the hands of dacoits.

With much reluctance I must tell you that his file is officially closed.

His personal belongings and last will and testament are being forwarded to his family who I am sure will be in touch with you in due course.

May I offer you my sincere condolences.

I remain your most obedient servant,

   Sir George Haskin
      Secretary of State for India

Ronnie reached for the next letter. It was different from the previous white, formal stiff envelopes of the India Office. This one was a softer, blue envelope with English stamps, postmarked Rugby, Warwickshire, 3 December 1927, and addressed to a Mrs Phyllis Elliott, Principal, St. Agnes' Teacher Training College, London.

Dear Mrs Elliott,

As you are an old friend of my mother's, I am taking the liberty of approaching you about the possibility of my becoming a teacher.

You may have heard that my fiancé, Henry Saville, the Assistant District Commissioner in Durgapur, U.P. India, disappeared last September and has now been officially presumed dead by the India Office.

Although in my heart of hearts I have difficulty in accepting this, especially in the absence of any evidence, I cannot continue being a financial burden on my father. Indeed, if I am to remake my life, it is imperative that I leave Rugby and try to start afresh.

Had I not been fortunate enough to meet and become engaged to Henry Saville, I would have taken up a scholarship to go to Somerville College, Oxford. Now with my future in disarray, it occured to me that I am at least qualified to apply for a teacher's training and that this would be the best way to reorganise my life.

I shall be in London on 14 December as Henry's solicitors wish to see me at 11.30 am. Is there any chance we could meet that afternoon?

I would be so grateful for your time and advice.

I look forward to your reply,

With best wishes,

Yours sincerely,

Isabella Mayne.

LETTER TO MISS ISABELLA MAYNE FROM MRS ELLIOTT,
REGENT'S PARK, LONDON
7 DECEMBER 1927

Dear Isabella,

So very sorry to hear of this tragedy. Of course I'll do my utmost to help. Can you come to St. Agnes' at four o'clock? We can have a long talk over tea in my lodgings.

If I don't hear further, I shall expect you then.

Warmest regards,

Phyllis Elliott.

The next envelope was pink and had a cluster of roses in the corner. Ronnie frowned. Who could that be? As he slid out the pale pink sheet a waft of rose scent escaped into the air. Rose scent, trapped for fifty years? Ronnie shuddered and almost looked behind him as if the scent could somehow invoke the person who had sent the letter. He looked at the signature: Gwendoline – of course. Aunty Gwen! He'd been to tea with her once in Hampstead. He'd managed to knock his milk all over her beautiful white lace tea cloth, and had been sent out on to the heath in disgrace with the maid. He shrugged at the memory, then read on.

LETTER TO MISS ISABELLA MAYNE FROM MISS
GWENDOLINE LANDLESS
19 DECEMBER 1927

Dearest Izzie,

(Ronnie couldn't help smiling. Yes, Aunt Gwen used to call his grandmother Izzie. To the fury of Grandfather.)

My poor darling. What a frightful time you've had. I think it's a ripping notion for you to go to St. Agnes'. It's only a twenty-minute tram ride from here, you know, so Izzie darling, look no further for digs. Come and share my flat with me. It's easily big enough. You'd have your own bedroom and we share the kitchen and bathroom with one other girl – Maisie Foster. She's a good sort and I'm sure we would all get along famously.

Why not stay a night or two and see for yourself?

Write immediately and say you will.

Your ever ever loving friend,

Gwendoline.

Yes, but what happened to Grandfather? Impatiently, Ronnie skimmed through the next two or three letters; Isabella had obviously come to London to study at St. Agnes' and moved into digs with her friend, Gwendoline; blue . . . pink . . . blue envelopes then suddenly, white. A large, thick white envelope. Ronnie snatched at it and as he did, a crumpled piece of brown paper fluttered to the floor. He fumbled. Almost ignored it. Picked it up and realised it was a telegram, so creased, as if it had been handled, fingered, pressed into pockets, folded and unfolded many times. He smoothed it out.

'DURGAPUR UP 4 JANUARY
DELIGHTED TO INFORM YOU HENRY SAVILLE ALIVE
AND WELL STOP MORE DETAILS FOLLOWING STOP
JAMES RICHMOND

Outside, a misty darkness had settled on the city. The orange
street lamps glowed, disembodied. Ronnie closed the curtains.
He didn't glance back at his grandfather. He wouldn't see him
anyway. Outside the quivering, fringed circle of light the
darkness in the room spread away intense and silent. It
demolished all walls and boundaries, and extended seamless,
black, infinite, out and out into the universe.

Only he, Ronnie, orbiting on his own planet existed and
those about whom he would now read in the thick, white
envelope.

3

FOUND

LETTER TO MISS ISABELLA MAYNE FROM HENRY SAVILLE
6 JANUARY 1928 DURGAPUR

My dearest, sweet Isabella,

I trust you have received by telegraph the news that I am alive!

Yes, my darling, it is I, feeling a little like Rip Van Winkle, stumbling back to my people and my loved ones. I can only humbly kneel before God and thank Him for my deliverance, and for answering the only prayer I had, that I might return to England and marry you.

Forgive me for the pain I must have caused you. I pray God that you forgive me.

Last year before we parted, we pledged to marry next Easter when I would be home on leave. I hope and pray that you still love me, for I wish more than anything to continue with those plans. Dearest, telegraph me and say that you will. Until I know that you are still a part of my life, I will not feel truly restored home.

I intend booking a passage on P&O sometime round 8 March. I will send you more precise details when I know them. In the meantime, dear Isabella, could you, would you speak to the Reverend Ealy and discuss a possible date for our marriage?

This news would do more than anything to help me recover my senses and well-being, for I have had the strangest time these last months. I will do my best to tell you about them so that you are not embarrassed by any other garbled versions which might reach your ears.

It all began on the evening of 9 September. I was sitting alone on my verandah having an evening smoke before retiring to bed. My

19

servant, Ram Singh, was away for two days visiting his sick mother. The other servants were dismissed for the night and were in the servants' quarters. I could hear them singing and drumming round their charcoal burner, getting a little tipsy on fermented rice water. It was a night like any other.

Then suddenly a voice called to me softly, out of the darkness. 'Sahib!' I could see no one and cried, 'Who's there? Show yourself!'

'Sahib will stay quiet please,' ordered the voice. 'I have information. You have reward?'

He was referring to my much-publicised call for information about a gang of dacoits who have been terrorising this area for months.

'My information is good. Come with me tonight. Now, alone, and I will take you to the dacoit camp.' The man in the darkness spoke in an insistent whisper.

Until that moment I had been frozen to my seat, now I jumped up and strode to the edge of the verandah trying to catch a glimpse of the man. I felt nervous and exposed in the verandah light and angry that anyone should think I could just get up and go out into the night with an unknown man. It was crazy.

'Tell me your information first,' I cried.

I heard the faintest rustle then nothing. What a bungler I was. I cursed my stupidity. This was the first time anyone had offered information and I had all but turned it down. I returned to my chair and sat down, once more fully exposed in the verandah light. I lit my pipe and tried to look unafraid. If the man was serious, surely he would come back. As I waited, my mind was racing. If he came back, if he was telling the truth and he could lead me to the dacoits, what plan should I formulate? Whom could I tell? Could I trust him?

Could he trust me, is probably what he was thinking, poor man. Dacoit reprisals are terrible and the prime reason why we had had no lead whatsoever till now. Even though I have ridden constantly into the villages, talked to the elders, promised them armed protection from the garrison, tried to give them confidence, I have failed to penetrate the barrier of fear which these dacoits have put up. The dacoits have a hold everywhere. We can't even be sure our own servants aren't lookouts and informants for them. So while I was worrying about the danger I might be in, I knew that if he was serious his danger was infinitely worse.

I puffed casually on my pipe then said in a low, clear voice, 'If what you say is true then your reward will be great. I can give you fifty rupees tonight if you will lead me to the camp and another fifty if we are able to get soldiers out to capture them.'

'It is agreed.' The voice seemed almost at my elbow and I nearly jumped out of my skin. 'You get the money, please, but do not attract any attention. If anyone is alerted, the deal is off. When you have the money come back on to the verandah just as you are. Keep smoking your pipe.'

Trying to look normal, I got up and wandered back into the bungalow. The safe was in my office and, out of the glare of the verandah light, I stood for a moment in the darkness torn by indecision. Was I mad to go with a total stranger, a man whose face I hadn't even seen, a disembodied voice speaking in the night? But, Isabella, after all these months, this was the first lead. If this man was genuine and I didn't trust him, my offer would seem useless and no one would trust us again. I had to go. I took the money from the safe, downed a tot of whisky and sauntered back on to the verandah, puffing at my pipe as he had asked.

I stared into the darkness. Where was he? It seemed like an age before I heard his voice again. He told me to walk down to the main gate as if on an evening stroll. I was to keep smoking my pipe but at the gate I must put it out. 'The gate will be open,' he said.

'What about the chowkidar, the nightwatchman?' I asked. 'He always sits at the gate.'

'He has been dealt with,' said the voice. 'He will sleep till morning.'

So I did as he ordered. Isabella, the Hindus believe in Yama, God of the Dead and that he sends a messenger to fetch those chosen to die. As I moved towards the gate, I was filled with a strange premonition. Was this man *my* messenger of death? Did he carry a noose in his hand, as the Hindus believe, ready to trap my soul when it sprang from my body?

Rather than panic I felt utterly calm, totally at peace as if I were walking to my destiny. I turned once as if in farewell to look at my white-washed bungalow gleaming through the chequered shadows of the tamarind tree. The lamp on the verandah shone frail but brave, as if trying to reassure me that all I had to do was turn round and go back. The night was brimming with sound. Indian nights always are; crickets chirping, frogs croaking, insects teeming – suddenly masters of their universe. I could hear my servants

21

singing with voices slurred with drink and from an even greater distance, I could hear the drumming. How often I've cursed that sound, as every night, at the tomb of a local prophet, the guardian of the tomb drums to keep away evil spirits. Tonight the drumming comforted me and I knew there was no turning back.

I had never felt so much in the grip of this perplexing land. Here was I, coolly abdicating all my common sense, my English logic, my inbred superiority, to a native's voice in the night, the sound of drumming and the notion of Yama. I, who was taught leadership, was being led and I meekly followed in the sudden belief that I must succumb completely to whatever fate had in store for me.

When I reached the gate, it was open as my messenger had said. My old chowkidar, Sanjay, lay slumped on his bedroll, snoring like an old steam engine. I walked out on to the road then tapped my pipe against my boot to empty it of tobacco. The red sparks flew into the air before dropping into the dust. Now what?

'It is good.' The voice spoke softly just ahead of me. 'Follow the railway track in the down-train direction. You will reach a guava grove on the right-hand side. Go into it. I shall be there waiting with a horse.'

Now I saw him for the first time. He was only a smallish, thin man, draped, Indian style, in a dark cloak which he also used to cover his face. He looked too poor and ill at ease to be a messenger of Yama. Still, I called him my messenger and was prepared to do his bidding. The horse was no more impressive, it hardly looked capable of carrying one man, let alone two, but he mounted it and instructed me to climb on behind him. I felt we must have looked comical and pathetic as he urged the horse forward.

I have always prided myself in knowing my district like the back of my hand and for a while I did. Even in the darkness, I was familiar with the path we followed – out through the guava grove, on across the wide open fields of mustard then wheat. But soon the country became rougher and stonier. Our poor stumbling horse had to pick its way across ground pitted with holes, scrub and thorn bushes until we came to the course of a dried-up river bed. So long as we stayed with the river I still knew roughly where we were, but when my messenger abruptly changed direction and we began to wind our way through gulleys and twisting ravines, I began to lose track of myself. I tried to remember features of the landscape; I took note of a twisted tree, a pile of stones, the outline of an escarpment, but in the darkness everything merged into a blur.

'Why are you doing this?' I asked him. 'Aren't you in terrible danger?'

'They killed my wife and son,' he replied without emotion.

'How did you find their camp?' I asked.

'These things are known,' was all he would say.

So we rode on in silence. Now I had lost track of time as well. I had given up trying to remember the way and sometimes my head flopped on his back and I slept as the little horse rode on and on through the night. Suddenly, the horse stumbled and I awoke to find myself pitched to the ground. I heard a roaring sound and thought it was in my head, but it was the river. It had not dried up after all, merely changed course. I dragged myself to the edge of a ridge and looked down. My messenger came and stood beside me. 'Sahib all right?' he asked.

'Yes, yes!' I replied. 'But are we nearly there?'

'Another mile, perhaps,' he answered.

We both stared down, catching glimpses of white foam flickering in the darkness as the rushing water dashed its way among the boulders.

'We must go, Sahib,' the man urged me.

I knew he was right. There were not many hours left of the night. Wearily, I struggled back on to the horse.

The last part of the ride was so narrow and tortuous that anytime I expected to be hurled to the ground again. But the good little horse did not falter. Now we began to go down. Lower and lower we wound, sometimes squeezing between high, narrow rocks, or zig-zagging round huge boulders and sprawling thorn bushes. The last mile must have taken us nearly an hour. Then abruptly we halted. My messenger slid to the ground and instructed me to do the same. He tethered the horse and indicated that we were to climb a great rock face which sheered up ahead of us. I was about to protest but he leapt ahead of me and began to climb, finding one foothold after another as easily as if it were a ladder. I hurried to follow in his footsteps but I was gripped by doubt. Was this a trap? This man seemed to know his way so surely. Was he a dacoit? Had he persuaded me to take part in my own kidnapping?

But before I could go back, we reached the top. The rock flattened out like a table and we flopped on our stomachs, panting with exhaustion. For the first time, I saw my messenger's face. He turned towards me and his cloak dropped as he put a finger of warning to his lips. Taut, and shining with perspiration, his face was brimming with triumph. He pointed below and whispered, 'Dacoits!'

Do you know, Isabella, in that moment I felt a surge of pure happiness as I haven't felt since childhood. I don't know if you can possibly understand. It was like every schoolboy's dream come true: stalking through bandit country, led by a mysterious stranger, and now to be looking down on a camp-fire around which I knew were some of the most bloodthirsty men in the world. I had never felt more happy, more excited, more completely alive than I did then. The sky was black, as only an Indian sky can be, with that wild sprawl of stars scattered like diamonds across the universe.

In the flickering firelight I could make out at least a dozen bodies, sleeping Indian style with their blankets tucked under their feet and pulled up tightly right over their heads like shrouds. Tethered nearby were a dozen or so horses standing motionless like Greek statues. It was a scene of utter stillness, even beauty. But even as I indulged in such thoughts, uneasiness began to creep over me. Something was wrong. The scene was too still, too perfect. How could ruthless killers sleep: so vulnerable, so untroubled, so easy to capture? These were the most wanted men in the whole of the United Province and beyond. My excitement turned to terror. These men had to be well guarded!

I turned to my messenger just in time to see a flash of steel swoop down into my body. Simultaneously, another plunged into my poor companion. I think he died instantly.

I am not clear what happened next. I knew I was not dead and the searing pain which ripped through my back and into my chest almost comforted me. My sudden movement had deflected the knife away from my heart. My assailant hurled me over and would have plunged the knife in again, when he saw my face. My white face.

He gave a bloodcurdling roar! The shrouded bodies leapt into life, reaching for knives and rifles. Rough hands dragged me, pushed me, rolled me all the way down into their camp with screams of 'Ingrezi, Ingrezi! English!'

The sight of their pitiless faces leering at me jubilantly in the firelight gave me no hope. They prodded me with their rifles, kicked and spat at me. 'So, messenger,' I thought to myself, 'You were my messenger of death after all.'

I expected to die any moment, and I succumbed to the waves of unconsciousness, but they were not ready yet. They argued and quarrelled. Some were for finishing me off then and there, others for keeping me hostage. I just thought what fools they were. I would be dead anyway by the time they made up their minds for I was bleeding profusely.

There is now a gap in my life about which I can only speculate. Why was I not killed? Why was I not at the very least taken hostage for a ransom? Did they think I was dead already? Did they decide that I wasn't worth the risk of bringing down the wrath of the British police and army on to their heads? I will never know. The fact is I was left and then, by some miracle, I was found.

I have no idea how I came to be found or how long I lay in that deserted camp. James Richmond thinks it must have only been a few hours otherwise I would have bled to death. I have only fragments of memory and sensations.

I remember in my delirium seeing my dead messenger. His face was shining with the same triumphant expression I glimpsed before he was killed. He seemed to be beckoning me with one hand, while holding a slung noose with the other, the noose to catch my soul at the moment of death. My heart seemed to struggle in my chest, my spirit seemed to yearn to go with the messenger. Then I felt hands cushioning my head and untwisting my limbs. I didn't know if I was alive or dead. I remember cool, sweet water trickling down my throat, and a damp cloth wiping away the grime and blood from my face.

A face bent over mine and I thought it was yours. I think I called your name before I descended into a darkness from which I did not expect to return.

Time passed. Consciousness returned slowly in fragments of sensations. I heard a woman singing softly and the sound of a baby crying.

Blurred faces swam into my vision and out again – faces dark, Indian – an old, white-haired man, then a young, sad-faced woman. She bent low as she stroked my brow and cleaned my wounds. Once I opened my eyes to see the blue sky, broad green leaves, and branches twisting up above my head like the arched roof of some strange cathedral. 'I must be dead,' I thought, and fell back into oblivion.

Then one day I opened my eyes. My vision was clear and I felt awake – awake as if I had only gone to bed the night before and awoken after a deep untroubled sleep. I felt so calm and rested. I looked around me. There was the blue sky hanging like strange flowers down through the leaves of a tree. My sick bed was in the very heart of a tree, surrounded by coils of roots which thrust out of the ground. I heard that singing again, low and soft. I turned my head. It brought a stab of pain and my vision blurred again but still I struggled to see and realised I was looking at a young girl. She squatted just outside my curious sick room, grinding spices on a stone and she sang as she rocked to and fro. From time to time, she tipped a small clay pot into her hand and dashed water on to the stone then worked it into the spices to create a dark, red paste. A delicate smell of herbs and spices rose into the air and I felt hungry. Then I heard a bleating, like a goat, I thought, until I saw a bundle of rags lying quite close to the girl and a tiny, naked baby kicked and waved its feeble, brown limbs in the sunshine.

Soundlessly I watched this gentle scene. This was India, this was life carrying on as usual and I was alive.

Memory came filtering back. With a sickening lurch I remembered the dacoits, the flashing knife; death!

I cried out. I tried to sit up but dizziness made me roll over helplessly. The girl was at my side, looking at me with dark, frightened eyes.

'Police, police! We must fetch the police. Dacoits!' I cried.

The girl restrained me, pressing me back down on to my bed, soothing me in some strange dialect then she fled outside. A few moments later another figure appeared, bending low as he approached me among the roots.

It was the dark, white-haired old face of my delirium. Now I could see he was naked, except for a twist of saffron cloth twisted around his waist, and I knew he was a holy man. This old, wrinkled face looked down on me, so ancient and so wise that soon my agitation faded away under his penetrating gaze.

'My name is Henry Saville,' I said in Hindustani. 'I am Assistant District Commissioner for the Durgapur District. Who are you?'

'I serve Vishnu,' said the old man simply. One day, Isabella, I must try and explain all the Hindu gods to you. Vishnu is one of the great Hindu Trinity from which all other gods are supposed to stem. He is the Preserver and the Peacemaker and in those

26

moments I thanked God for a disciple of Vishnu who had helped to preserve my life and look after me in peace.

'Get help, get the police, the garrison!' I urged him but he pressed me back, and spoke in deep, authoritative tones.

'Don't worry yourself, Sahib. Forget things past, they are reduced to clay. Just sleep now and let the present reshape itself.' His eyes held mine for many moments until I slid away into unconsciousness once more.

Each time I slept, I never knew whether it was minutes, hours or days before I woke again. But with each waking I began to feel stronger. The old man and the girl were always there to offer me a bowl of curds, banana or freshly made chapatti. Each day they lifted me to wash my body and dress my wounds with their own preparations of herbs and forest bark. They cared for me with all the tenderness I might have expected had I been a son or a husband.

I was lying within a tree shelter made by roots like those I have often come across tracking in the forests. I have heard that hermits and holy men live in such dwellings for years. It is considered perfectly natural and commendable for a devout Hindu to retreat to the forest to perfect himself once he has fulfilled his role as son, husband and father. What is not common is that he is accompanied by a young girl and her baby.

Once when the old man was cleaning my wound, I watched the girl outside playing with her child. She looked no more than a child herself and when I caught her eye, it was like meeting the gaze of a frightened animal and she turned quickly, scooped up her baby and disappeared. I wondered about her and what she was doing here. As if he had seen, as if he could read my thoughts, the old man said, 'She is my daughter.'

'Why do you not fetch help?' I asked him. 'I must be a burden to you and your daughter.'

The old man, frail though he appeared, easily lifted me into a sitting position, and held a clay cup of curds to my lips.

'Why do you not tell the authorities I am here. They will be looking for me.' I felt my voice rising with anger, and tears fell down my face.

'Ah! You think you need finding, do you?' the old man murmured sweetly as he took the cup away and laid me down. 'Why do you worry about such things? Why not find yourself first and then let others find you?' He wiped away my tears with the edge of his robe and pressed his fingers to my temple, intoning sacred words as he did so. His voice droned on and on till my rage subsided and I felt my limbs unclench and peace creep over me.

But though he calmed and tried to reassure me I knew what a sacrifice they must be making to keep me here and feed me. God knows the poverty of most of the people in this land. To live alone like this, in the middle of the jungle, is to tread an infinitely fragile line between gathering enough to eat and starving. A hermit alone might manage but a young woman and a baby as well as myself – it wasn't possible.

'Where is her husband?' I asked.

His hand trembled slightly as he took it away from my head. He got up and moved over to the entrance of the den where he could stand upright. I thought he would leave without answering but he suddenly turned and said, 'Her husband is dead but I would not let them burn her.'

4
SUTTEE

Dear Isabella, it was with such joy that I heard the old man's words. In a way it sums up the giant puzzle that India is to many of us. One moment you are marvelling at the gentleness, beauty and compassion of her people, and the next you are suddenly faced with death and what seems like needless brutality, all the worse for seeming so incomprehensible. Disease is terrible but we understand it as an affliction outside ourselves, if you like. Even robbery, terrorism and the dacoits we understand as part of man's desire for power and his greed for wealth, but when you come up against a custom like suttee, it is like falling into an abyss in human thought; a blank; an unknowing.

I actually saw suttee only once, three years ago, when I was still new to India. I was hunting with Ram Singh, my bearer and friend, in the forest on the trail of a killer tiger, and it led us close to a village on the other side of a river. We thought we'd find rest and food in the village, when we saw a funeral pyre on the banks.

This was no moment to intrude. We tethered our horses and squatted discreetly within the fringe of the jungle to watch. We heard chanting voices and the excited babble of children then a procession of men appeared from between the simple dung and thatched huts of the village. They carried a stretcher on which lay a white-swathed corpse.

They continued down to the river's edge where a priest greeted them with prayers. The pall-bearers waded into the water and immersed the body, while the chant of prayers grew louder and more intense. Finally they carried the body over to the funeral

29

pyre where a ladder was used to lift up the stretcher and slide it into position on a specially built platform.

The crowd and mourners formed a tight semi-circle at a suitable distance from the pyre, and someone appeared with a burning torch. Others circled the pyre tossing ghee, clarified butter, on to the wood, partly as a gift to the gods, and partly to help the fire burn more fiercely. At a given signal, a young boy was pushed forward from the crowd. He was weeping.

'We are watching the funeral of a man from this village,' whispered Ram Singh, 'and this boy must be his son. It is the duty of the eldest son to light the funeral pyre otherwise the father's soul cannot go to Heaven.'

At that moment the flaming torch was thrust into the young boy's hand. He staggered a little but then he seemed to take hold of himself and with great dignity held the torch to the fat-drenched wood. Within seconds tall flames leapt into the air with a great spitting and crackling. Soon the platform was consumed by fire. As the wood burned away, the platform bearing the body sank lower and lower on the pyre. I watched with morbid fascination as the corpse blackened in the heat.

Suddenly the body moved and twisted as if in pain. It seemed to rise as if trying to sit up. I cried out in horror. 'My God! He's alive!' I would have rushed forward. But Ram Singh held me back. 'No, Sahib,' he cried.'It is just the effect of the heat.'

No sooner had I got over this shock, when a chilling shriek rang out above the noise of prayers and fire and weeping. It was a shriek more terrible than anything I had ever heard. The young son, still clasping the brand seemed transfixed with horror. As if in response to a signal, the tight semi-circle of mourners parted just enough to allow a group of people through into the arena. At first I thought this was just another group of mourning relatives. The women were wailing in a high-pitched drone as they do in India as a kind of social support for the grief of the bereaved. But then I realised that they were half dragging, half carrying a young woman towards the flames.

Ram Singh clasped my arm. 'Sahib! Let's go!' he urged. He tried to pull me away into the trees.

'Why?' I shook him free. 'What is happening now?'

'It is the widow,' he replied quietly. 'Please, Sahib, let's go.'

I did not understand the full meaning of his words. It all happened so quickly. The group dragged the woman towards the burning pyre until they were stopped by the blast of heat upon their faces. They thrust the woman forwards and fell back into the circle of mourners, who closed ranks and formed a tight circle. There was no way through.

Like some terrified animal caught in a forest fire, the young woman turned this way and that, her shrieks turned to pitiful high-pitched squeaks. But when she saw no hope from the wall of faces, she threw up her arms and hurled herself on to the burning corpse of her husband.

The flames caught her saree and there was a brilliant surge of green and yellow fire. A huge moan of satisfaction rose from the crowd, drowning my anguished howl of fury and disbelief.

Why, why, why? I would have leapt among them in my rage and consternation but Ram Singh pulled me back into the forest and tried to make me understand.

'Without a husband, her life is over. She would be an outcaste, refused food and shelter. She would have no place to go. It is best to have done what she has done.'

'But where is love?' I cried. 'Love of fathers, brothers, sons, family? What happens to love?'

No answers he gave me could make me understand. So you see, Isabella, when this Hindu holy man, this devout Hindu, could turn to me and say of his daughter, "I would not let them burn her," I felt an indescribable joy that after all there is love, a love and compassion that is prepared to transcend the boundaries of custom, race and creed.

From that day on, I asked my rescuers no more questions. The quicker I recovered my health, the quicker I would cease to be a burden on them.

Once I had stopped fighting with impatience; stopped trying to take action, my days were full of deep serenity. At last I could walk unaided to the edge of the clearing and look at the great tree which had been my shelter. Now I could wash and dress myself, but I could also guard the fire while the old man and his daughter went out into the jungle in search of food. They also trusted me to look after the baby, stir the cooking pot, fan away the insects and ward off other predators drawn to the clearing by the smell of food.

It was a time of great peace and tranquillity. I felt in a kind of limbo, reduced to the utmost simplicity of action and thought. Somehow I no longer wanted to think about the day when I would be well enough to leave. Life seemed so perfectly balanced; so far from the idiotic convolutions and torments that man outside seems so good at creating for himself.

It was not I who decided I was ready. I knew I was stronger; strong enough to carry firewood, to walk some distance into the forest, to be up a whole day without tiring. Yet I felt content to stay forever. I viewed all my past life, you, my family, my job, as if they were part of some distant dream. I was reluctant to go home and face up to my responsibilities.

But the old man was wiser than I. One evening after we had eaten supper round the fire, he said quietly, 'My son, tomorrow you must go home.'

My eyes filled with tears, I knelt at his feet to beg him to let me stay, but he raised me up and looked through my tears with such authority that I bowed my head and said meekly, 'Yes, if it must be so.'

He woke me before daybreak. The shrill cry of peacocks had not yet pierced the darkness, and no bird rustled in anticipation of the dawn. The old man placed my boots at my feet – I had not worn them since I came into the forest. He held out my jacket for me to put on. When I was dressed, I followed him outside. The girl was waiting for me. I could just make out her slight shape huddled in a shawl.

I hesitated. I didn't know how to say 'goodbye'. I didn't know how to thank them. How could I just leave? How could I show them the love I had learned to feel for them?

I still had the fifty rupees in my pocket which had been intended for my poor messenger, but what use was money to them in the forest? I felt again in my pocket, and my fingers closed over my pocket watch. Instinctively, I knew this is what I could give. The watch was of no great monetary value, but it was a handsome object with a gold chain and I treasured it. It had been left to me by my grandfather. His initials, the same as mine, were engraved on its silver back. H.R.S.

I lifted it out and held it dangling in the soft firelight, then I walked quietly to a hollow within the roots of the tree where I knew the baby was sleeping. I slipped the watch and chain round his neck and prayed with all my heart that somehow it would protect him from danger.

I went back to the old man. He stood so still and sad that I was sure that he had learned to love me too. I knelt down and kissed his feet. He placed his hands on my head and murmured a prayer, '*Rām Rām Sita Rām*,' then raised me to my feet.

'Go now with my daughter,' he said. 'She will lead you to a path near the river. Once on this path, follow it for many miles. It may rise and fall and go in many directions but in the end it will lead you to the railway track. Here, you will turn to the north and follow the railway. It is far but you are strong now and in two days you will reach Durgapur.'

As we set off, a tremor ran through the forest and the first pink rays of dawn pierced through the tangled undergrowth in brilliant shafts. Green parrots rose like a dark cloud, shrieked with joy, and swooped up into the heavens. Wild peacocks now emerged from the undergrowth, sleepy but dazzling, they preened and strutted in the dappled light. Monkeys awoke with an instant babble, whooping and bounding through the trees and a shy mongoose gaped at us with startled eyes before coiling up a tree and disappearing into the leaves.

We walked, the daughter and I, until the sun was high above us. We eased our hunger and thirst by plucking fruit but never stopped to rest until we suddenly, miraculously, came upon the path.

The girl touched my arm shyly and pointed. I nodded and translated her silent message. 'This path will lead me home,' I said.

She nodded. 'Home, home.' Then as if afraid of farewells, she rapidly folded her hands together, bent down and lightly kissed my feet, and then was gone.

A feeling of utter desolation swept over me. I would have sunk to the ground and wept but my instinct for survival took over. A jungle is no place to linger alone and unarmed. If I did not keep moving, I might not reach the railway track before night and that was vital. I began to whistle and sing and shout your name. The spell of the forest was weakening. I began to think of home.

5

THE PROPHECY

Dearest Isabella,

You will be aware that you are not the only one pleading with me to return to England immediately to recover from what so many insist on calling "my dreadful experience".

No doubt you have heard comments about how I lived with natives for too long; that I am not quite right in the head; that I have somehow been corrupted.

But you of all people must understand. Has not my last letter fully described what happened? You know that my experience was something more mystical, more far-reaching than anything I have ever known? And I must warn you, dearest, the matter is not yet over as I will now try and explain.

Just as I knew when I followed my messenger that I was going into unknown territory – even the land of death – so it is that I know that what I am going to tell you is to take us both – yes, I mean you, too – into the unknown territory of our most private feelings, emotions, prejudices, hopes and fears. On that night I abdicated myself to fate – and I mean fate in the Eastern sense – of being mobilised in a design greater than ourselves. Now it is with a sense of fate continuing to work its pattern that I tell you what happened next.

I had to go to Lucknow, the local government seat, to hand in my report about the dacoits and answer questions on what had happened to me and to see whether my information was going to be of any use in tracking down the dacoits. Alas, I'm afraid it was not. I retraced the route my messenger and I took but there was no trace of them. To my sorrow, we found only the remains of a

34

funeral pyre on the banks of the river, and I can only assume that the good holy man and his daughter had performed the last rites over my poor messenger, committed his body to the flames and scattered his ashes into the river. I hope his soul is at peace.

The interview was long and exhausting and when at last I was free to go, I found myself drawn to walk aimlessly into the bazaar until it was time to catch the train back to Durgapur.

I left my tonga waiting for me on the outskirts and plunged into the noisy, exotic bustle of tightly packed stalls and narrow streets. The sun had set by now and the shopkeepers had lit their kerosene lamps and hung them from the rickety structures of their over-laden platforms. Voices hailed me like echoes from one side to another, 'Sahib! Sahib! You buy?'

But I let myself be jostled among the crowded shoppers, weaving in and out of ambling cows, picking my way over the bodies of half-starved dogs and ignoring the persistent, monkey-like fingers of curious children who followed me in my wake.

'Sahib!' A strangely high-pitched yet commanding voice arrested my attention. 'Here, Sahib!' The voice called again. It came from across the road. I pushed my way through the people to a saree stall. The silk and gold threads glistened in the kerosene light and the stall looked like a rajah's tent, it was so draped and hung with long swathes of brightly coloured sarees. Then I saw him. My heart stood still. At first glance he looked like my holy man. A small, thin dark figure, he stood in his saffron robes, a begging bowl in one hand, and a stick taller than himself in the other.

Our eyes met and held. I was confused. This was not my holy man. I felt a fool. India is full of holy men and soothsayers, who make a fortune out of waylaying gullible characters to sell them prayers or tell their horoscopes. I pretended I had not seen him and began to examine the sarees. The shopkeeper eagerly flung one glittering saree after another across the floor.

'Sahib!' The strange high-pitched voice spoke again. 'You will gain a son before you gain a wife.'

I turned with astonishment, half-amused, half-angry. But the man had gone. I could just make out the tip of his stick moving farther and farther away through the crows. I shrugged and looked at the shopkeeper. If he had heard, he knew better than to show it.

At first I dismissed the words as impudence then I brooded about them on the train home that night. I managed to joke about them briefly in the club the next day, then I forgot about them.

Three days ago was my day for distributing rice and flour to the natives from the surrounding villages. It is always done from my bungalow to ensure that people can buy their staple food at honest government prices, instead of being cheated by the black marketeers. It is one of my duties that I really enjoy. The villagers came by camel and bullock cart from many miles around and by nine o'clock in the morning the compound was crowded. It is an uncommonly handsome sight to see the women in their vivid-coloured skirts, heavily bejewelled in all their finery for it is an important social occasion for them. They come with their babies and cooking pots, and bedrolls and they come with their gossip and news to spread round the rest of the district.

Ram Singh and I use two huge pairs of scales with iron weights. As each person queues up, we weigh the requisite amount of rice and flour into their outspread squares of cloth which they then tie, corner to corner, and balance on their heads for the long trek home.

Thus we worked all through the day till our backs and arms ached with bending and weighing. By dusk we had cleared almost everyone from the compound. Ram Singh weighed the last bundle of flour and I the last of the rice.

'That's it!' I sighed, and collapsed the scales ready to put away until next time.

'Wait, Sahib!' cried Ram Singh. 'There is one left, over there.' He pointed to a spot beyond the tamarind tree. 'I will check.'

Someone was sitting in a huddle with arms clasped around the knees and head buried inside a shawl. Ram Singh tapped the person. Although I saw no movement or response, something must have been said, for Ram Singh came hurrying back.

'Sahib,' he frowned looking puzzled. 'It is an old lady. She will not go away and insists on speaking to you. She asked for you by name.'

I groaned. We often get all sorts of people coming with grievances or petitions about one thing or another and I felt too tired to deal with what was probably some family dispute.

'Shall I get the other servants to remove her?' asked Ram Singh, seeing my reluctance.

'She's old, you say?' I murmured.

'Yes, Sahib.'

'Well, we'd better deal with it, I suppose. Come with me.'

Together we walked over to the still shape.

'Old woman,' I spoke to her in Hindi. 'Have you purchased your ration of flour and rice?'

There was no answer. She did not move. 'Old woman,' I repeated, 'what do you want?'

Suddenly she raised her head, and a scrawny, wizened arm pulled back the shawl from her face. What an old, brown, creased face it was, with dark, leaden eyes and a resigned expression. She spoke faintly and slowly, as though knowing I would not understand her dialect. Ram Singh translated.

'She says she is a messenger.'

Mark that, Isabella, a messenger. She used that word. My heart froze.

'She says she comes from a place of death but brings life. The message is that you should preserve this life as yours was preserved.'

She finished speaking and drew aside her shawl even more to reveal two bundles. I assumed they were her rice and flour but then she lifted one of the bundles up for me to take. It moved in my hands as I received it. Warily I pulled back the rags. Dear Isabella, how can I describe the horror, the fear, the totally primitive desire to fling the bundle away and run? For in my arms I held a young baby whose naked body was completely covered in smallpox.

I found myself shouting. 'Ram Singh! Fetch the doctor immediately. Round up as many people as possible who were in the compound. Send servants after those who have left for home. Bring them all back. This is smallpox. If we do not catch them now the whole district could become infected. Everyone must be vaccinated immediately.'

At the sound of my voice, all my servants came running. Ram Singh roared out instructions and fled. I gently laid the baby down on the ground within the spread of the old woman's shawl and told her to stay there. Then, almost fainting, I staggered back to my bungalow yelling for hot water and disinfectant. I washed and scrubbed my whole body over and over again, until I had regained my composure.

Of course there was a terrible pandemonium. People crowded into the compound yelling and shouting. Within twenty minutes, Dr Bailey came at a gallop in his tonga, with bag in hand and three nurses in tow. The old woman and the baby were immediately examined.

'Damn!' he muttered. 'It's smallpox all right.' He ordered the nurses to set about vaccinating everyone while he accompanied the two victims back to hospital.

All through the night we worked, rounding up villagers, organising them into lines, vaccinating them, and then allotting them a place in the compound where they could bed down for the night as we could not now send them out into the darkness.

All through the night the nurses worked without rest, filling and refilling their syringes, vaccinating the anxiously held-out arms. The servants and I organised vast quantities of tea and I ordered dhal and chapattis to be prepared.

It was nearly noon the next day before the whole operation was complete and the last of the villagers had been vaccinated and sent home.

At last, red-eyed and exhausted, the nurses collected everything up, clambered wearily into a tonga and went home. I dismissed Ram Singh for the day and then I, too, fell into bed and slept for the next ten hours.

Two days later, I was having my breakfast on the verandah as usual, when a tonga was admitted through the compound gates and came trotting up to the front of the house. It was Dr Bailey, accompanied, to my surprise, by Miss Murray, one of the missionaries attached to St. Mary's Church. I invited them to join me.

Dr Bailey came straight to the point. 'Mr Saville, I understand that during the weeks you were declared missing and believed dead, you were in fact being cared for and sheltered by two natives in the forest.'

'That is correct,' I replied, dreading that I must go over my story again for the fiftieth time.

'I also understand from James Richmond that you refuse to divulge the whereabouts of these two people or give any idea of the location in which they sheltered you for fear of reprisals.'

'That is true,' I nodded.

'May I hazard a guess, Mr Saville,' said Dr Bailey, leaning forward in a confidential manner, which also contained a glimmer of triumph. 'May I hazard a guess that the two natives who rescued you were an old holy man and his widowed daughter?'

I gasped.

'And did his daughter have a young baby?' he asked.

'How did you know?' I exclaimed.

Without answering, Dr Bailey felt in his pocket and pulled out a watch and chain. He handed it to me. 'I think this may be yours,' he said gently.

I took it as if in a dream, and turned it over in my palm. Yes, there on the back were my grandfather's initials, H.R.S. There was no doubt.

I held the watch and a multitude of thoughts and memories flooded through my mind.

'But how . . .?' I asked, mystified. Then gasped with horror.'Not the baby,' I cried. 'Not the baby with smallpox.'

Dr Bailey nodded. He seemed surprised at my distress.

'Look,' he said tapping my knee. 'The baby's probably going to pull through. It was a near thing but it survived the night so I think the worst is over. The old woman though, I'm afraid she was not so lucky. She died early this morning.'

'Who was she?' I asked. 'There was no old woman in the forest.'

'The old woman was an untouchable who lived on the outskirts of a village on the edge of the forest. It seems there was an outbreak of smallpox. People fled into the jungle hoping to escape the disease but actually they took it with them and your old man and his daughter caught it. The old man died first.

'When the daughter knew that she, too, had it, she struggled towards the village and just managed to deliver the child into the hands of the old woman. Before she died, she instructed the old woman to take the baby to you and promised her that she would be well-rewarded by you.'

I bowed my head with anguish and thought of the lovely young daughter and the old man who had given me a small glimpse of paradise. It was unbearable to think they had suffered. How it hurt me, too, to imagine the long struggle it must have been for that courageous girl to reach the village.

'I was with the old woman when she died,' Dr Bailey went on. His voice was now not so triumphant and smug as he realised my distress.

'Did she say anything?' I asked.

'There were only two things she kept repeating. The first was, "He must preserve this life as his was preserved." '

'Yes,' I recalled. 'That's what she said to me in the compound. And what else?'

'She had this bundle,' said Dr Bailey, 'which she said you had not taken.'

39

'The first bundle was the baby,' I agreed. 'But what was in the second bundle?'

'I'll fetch it for you. I left it in the tonga for the moment.' Dr Bailey got to his feet. 'Don't worry, by the way. We took the liberty of destroying the original cloth in which they came and disinfecting the contents.'

He returned carrying a bulky cloth bundle which he placed before me on the table. 'Sorry to poke my nose into your affairs like this, old chap,' he apologised. 'Necessary precautions and all that!'

I undid the knots and folded back the cloth. There stood three metal bowls of three different sizes.

'Is that all?' I gazed at them, puzzled. I tipped them over and looked inside, but they were empty. They just seemed to be ordinary household pots.

'The old woman insisted that these pots belonged to the child and that he must never be parted from them,' explained Dr Bailey. 'Rum business, eh? Wouldn't take it too seriously if I were you. Cooking pots mean more to these poor people than you'd imagine. But no value, that's for sure. Sorry to burden you with it.'

'Preserve this life,' I murmured almost to myself.

'Of course, Mr Saville,' broke in Miss Murray, speaking for the first time, 'you shall do no such thing, er . . . directly, I mean. I have taken the liberty of coming with Dr Bailey to inform you that we can admit this child immediately into the mission orphanage. He will be well looked after, well preserved –' she gave a prim laugh at her own little joke. 'He will get a good Christian education, and a better chance in life than if he had not been orphaned. That is so often the case.' She sighed piously. 'Of course, if you could make some kind of contribution towards his upkeep, that will more than fulfil your obligation towards his mother and grandfather.'

'I think I can decide how much of an obligation I feel, Miss Murray,' I spoke furiously and she flushed with anger. But my dislike of the woman was intense. I addressed Dr Bailey. 'The baby is in hospital for the moment in your care, is he not?' I asked.

'Oh yes, at least for another week. We will not discharge him to anyone until he is thoroughly fit.'

'Then I will let you know in due course what I decide,' I said firmly. I thanked them both for their concern though Miss Murray still looked deeply offended, and waved them off again in their tonga.

When the gates closed behind them I sat down at the table once more and arranged the three bowls in front of me. I felt a deep sadness and sense of loss and stroked the bowls as if they would link me for a few moments with my friends. But I was puzzled, too. What was their significance? They must have been an almost intolerable added burden for the girl to carry. The more I thought about it, the more disturbed I felt.

I ran my fingers round their metal bodies, felt their cool texture and solidity.

There was something different, I was sure. These were not like any crude cooking pots. There was no sign that they had been put on a fire or had ever contained food. They were polished and smooth and finely – even lovingly wrought. I touched them, smoothed them, as if somehow they would tell me why they were so important.

Almost by accident, I ran my finger round the rim of the largest bowl and a low hum began to sound. I went on, pressing a little harder, as if it were a wine glass. The hum got louder and stronger and after a while as I continued to rub the rim faster and harder, the hum seemed to change its voice. Other vibrations joined in producing a droning effect.

It throbbed through my fingers, up my arms, into my face, into the very bone structure of my head.

It was hypnotic. It was overwhelming, in turns exciting, comforting, pleasurable and communicative.

I began to stroke the other bowls and found I could produce similar effects. Later that night I sat with my bowls allowing my senses to be immersed in these beautiful sounds. It seemed to liberate all my thoughts and feelings so that when, finally, I stopped, it was because I knew quite clearly what I must do.

The old woman's message was unmistakable – and the will of the old man and his daughter irrefutable. 'Preserve this life as yours was preserved.' Me. I must do it. Not Miss Murray and the mission. Not anyone else. Me. It was my life for his life. My path was clear, my decision fixed.

You see, Isabella, the holy man in Lucknow was right: I have gained a son before I have gained a wife.

I can only pray to God, fate, whatever forces are within the universe, that having gained my son, you are the wife I will gain thereafter.

6

WHITE MOTHER,
BROWN CHILD

'Ronnie!'

Ronnie was several decades away, back in time, sitting with
his grandfather on a verandah in India. His grandfather was a
young man, Henry Saville. Ronnie had seen photographs of
him, tall, lean, wearing shorts, posed with a rifle near a slain
tiger. Now he sat with him at the table with the three metal
bowls. His ears were full of the humming as Henry Saville ran
his finger round the rims and strange resonances rose into the
air.

'Ronnie!' His mother's sharp, whispered voice broke into his
thoughts. It jerked him back to reality with a shock. Back to
the darkened bedroom and the small, fringed circle of light in
which he crouched as he read the papers.

Quickly, Ronnie gathered up the newspaper cuttings and
letters as he heard her light step approaching on the stairs. He
dropped them hurriedly into the briefcase and pushed it
behind the curtain. Now was not the time to go over the past
with his mother. He didn't even know if she knew about the
briefcase. He felt resentful at being disturbed. He felt as if for
the past hour he had been sitting in a time machine. Like a
ghost from the future, he had been at his grandfather's side,

being led by fate to an encounter with the child who would be his father one day.

Soon, so soon, he would understand who he really was. It would wipe away the pretence that he was simply Ronnie Saville, born without a past to his mother, Linda Margaret Pearcy, and (here the deception as Ronnie saw it) Adam Manu Saville.

Now he knew something of his great-grandfather, the holy man in the forest; and his real grandmother, the young girl who had cared for Henry Saville, and the baby, his father, known only to the world as Adam Manu Saville.

He sighed with impatience and started on some homework seconds before his mother appeared in the doorway. It always forestalled inevitable recriminations if he could look as though he had been working.

'Everything OK?' she asked in a breathless voice. Ronnie looked up casually.

'Fine,' he replied shortly. She was looking pretty and flushed. He wondered if that bloke, Mike, had seen her home. He felt a surge of resentment. She had been doing herself up recently. In fact, whereas before she had been content to spend most of her life in shabby jeans with her long, brown hair drawn lazily back in a pony-tail, now she had had her hair chopped to shoulder length and layered stylishly, and she had taken to wearing trim, figure-hugging skirts, and flouncy blouses. She bored him to tears with her sudden obsession for dieting and calorie counting and had added yet another night out in the week to attend Weight Watchers. Still, he had to admit she was looking slimmer and it suited her.

'Grandpa's right,' thought Ronnie. 'She is still young – and pretty.' His eyes softened with admiration. He felt an impulse to leap up and hug her but he couldn't. They had lost the habit of touching each other. He remembered how embarrassed he used to feel if his mother kissed him or touched him in front of his friends, even if it was to straighten his tie or brush some dandruff from his collar. They had rowed about it and in the end she had stopped.

Now they seemed to row about everything and he was often horribly rude, calling her names which later filled him with remorse and made him want to rush back and say he loved her. But he never could.

Gradually, they grew apart. She accepted that he was no longer a child. He was as tall as a man, taller than her Mike, yet he was only sixteen and sometimes Ronnie felt very like a child.

She began going out more, having boyfriends. Suddenly, he withdrew into his hobbies and school friends, and spent more and more time with his grandfather. When his grandfather became ill, Ronnie had slipped into an easy and absorbed companionship with him. They had always been close. With his grandfather, he had barely felt the loss of his father. Henry Saville had done everything a father could have done and even as much as many a mother. He worked so tirelessly in the house and garden that his age seemed irrelevant and his life everlasting. Somehow, he had always been around when Ronnie needed him, and more importantly, had always done things with him.

Ronnie glanced round. It was hard to believe that only a few months ago his grandfather had been the vigorous, tall man he had known all his life; helping him mend bicycle punctures, going on long walks and bike rides together, camping out in the countryside and teaching him all the skills of childhood. But as Ronnie grew older it was his grandfather's quiet wisdom he learned to admire. He became the yardstick against which everything was measured. 'When he dies, to whom will I turn?'

He thought of Old Father Time with scythe in hand. Grandfather had been tall and upright all his life, as tall as stalks of wheat in the wheatfield, only to be struck to the ground as if by an invisible scythe, which had swiped through his life and left him dying. Ronnie felt a rush of panic.

44

'Mum!'

'Sssh! Don't wake him yet,' she whispered, pleadingly. 'I'd like to get supper done with before I sort him out for the night.' She beckoned him to come downstairs.

Once in the kitchen, his mother began opening and shutting cupboard doors, and scouring through the fridge in an effort to produce a meal.

'You don't mind fish cakes and baked beans again, do you?' she asked ruefully.

'No, but only if you promise to do me one of your shepherd's pies tomorrow,' laughed Ronnie.

His mother looked up, surprised at his good humour. 'Of course, darling! I'll make you one of my very best,' then she stopped short, 'if . . .' she hesitated.

'If what,' sighed Ronnie, his irritation flooding back.

'If . . . well, what I'll do is prepare it before I go to work, and then when you get back from school, perhaps you could just pop it into the oven for me as I'll be late back.' She gave him a beguiling smile, tipped the baked beans into the saucepan and began stirring them dreamily.

'You see, I promised to meet Mike after work. He's going over one of the books I'm doing at my A Level evening class. You can manage that?'

'Yeah, suppose so,' muttered Ronnie, somehow disappointed.

'Don't you think I look slimmer?' she asked, changing the subject, and giving a twirl. 'I've lost six pounds already since I started Weight Watchers.'

'Yeah, you look great,' murmured Ronnie, unenthusiastically. He watched her thoughtfully as she slit open the packet of fish cakes and dropped them into a frying pan of sizzling fat.

'Mum, I'd like to go to India one day. Maybe soon,' Ronnie said brightly.

45

'What?' She turned, frowning at his words. She paused. 'Why India? It's a bit far, isn't it? There're lots of interesting places closer than that.'

'Why do you think?' retorted Ronnie, angrily.

'Now don't get rude.' Her voice rose.

'I'm not, but I make a perfectly normal remark, and you behave as though you're thick or something. What do you mean "why?" Don't you know why? Have you forgotten that you married an Indian? My father is Indian.'

'Your father wasn't Indian, except by race. He was as English as you or me. He never knew India.'

'Oh,' sneered Ronnie. 'He wasn't Indian. His skin was white, I suppose. Come off it, Mum. Was he English? Is that what others called him? Was he allowed to be English? Am I allowed to be English?' Ronnie was almost shouting now.

'Ronnie, just cool it! You shouldn't talk like that. Of course if you look for trouble you'll find it.'

'I don't look for trouble. I don't ask to be yelled at, Paki! Wog!'

His mother looked shocked and turned back to stirring the beans. 'It's only kids teasing. If you were fat you'd be fatty; if you wore glasses, you'd be specky-four eyes as I was at school. Surely you can take that?'

'Oh, I can take it. I can take it when I'm told to go back where I came from. Have you ever been told to go back where you came from? What am I supposed to do? Go back to Paddington? Is that where I came from? Oh, I can take it all right, but it's not the same and you should know that. When people jeer at the colour of your skin they jeer at everything about you. The hurt goes beyond just me; it hits you and Dad and my entire past and everything that I am. You're being naïve if you don't see the difference, or maybe dishonest, or maybe blind.'

Ronnie's words flowed faster and with passion. His blood was up, his heart thumping. Soon this conversation would end like most conversations with his mother: him yelling and walking out and she, first in tears then silent mortification, which could last for days. But he couldn't stop.

'Wars and riots haven't been caused by fatties versus thinnies! Spectacles versus eyes! They've been fought against race and colour. Apartheid isn't separate development of blondes from red-heads, is it?' His tone was bullying now. 'Is it, Mum? It's colour! Why don't you face up to it? Is it because deep down you're colour prejudiced, too? Would you like to forget you married an Indian? Perhaps you'd like to forget you produced a half-caste! Is that why you go out so much?' Ronnie finished up panting with fury, his voice harsh from shouting. He hardly felt the slap across his face.

'You always go too far!' cried his mother, her voice choked with misery and anger. She clenched her hands, desperately trying to control herself. 'I didn't leave your father, he left me, in a most cruel way. I loved him when I married him. I love you. I didn't do the rejecting, he did. I'm not rejecting you but you seem to be trying to tear me apart. I know it's a cruel world out there. I know there are racists. But don't stereotype me. Don't lump me in with them.'

There was a long silence while she turned back to the supper. She scraped the beans and fish cakes on to a plate and put it on the table. She reached for a bottle of coke and placed it near him. Ronnie knew it was her way of being conciliatory, though her hands still trembled and he could see the emotions still surging through her body.

He wanted to respond. 'Thanks,' he said gruffly and sat down to eat. He swallowed one bean at a time, stringing it out to give them both time to recover. But she didn't join him at the table. Instead, she went to the sink and began fiercely washing up the pans. He wondered if she was crying but she wouldn't turn her face towards him.

Feeling ashamed but helpless, Ronnie finished off his food. He took the plate over to the sink.

'All I said was that I'd like to go to India one day,' he said quietly. 'It's natural if you think about it. I'm sorry for what I said. I'll go up now and finish my homework.'

Ronnie climbed the stairs slowly. He felt calmer. He hadn't been brilliant but at least he'd managed to get out the word, "sorry". She wouldn't expect more.

As he entered his grandfather's bedroom, the old man's eyes glowed across the room like live coals. He had managed to heave himself up to a sitting position against his pillows. He raised his eyebrows questioningly as Ronnie went over to him.

'Yeah! Mum and me! We've been at it again,' murmured Ronnie, flopping dejectedly down on to the edge of the bed.

'You're too hard on her, old chap,' said the old man quietly.

'I know, I know,' cried Ronnie despairingly. 'But why can't she be more honest with herself? Sometimes she says things which betray not just me, or Dad, but you and even herself!'

'It's hard to think straight these days.' The old man sighed heavily. 'How can I show you the way things have changed. So drastically. Perhaps no other generation before has had to cope with such a change in values and priorities as my generation has had to and all in one lifetime. How can I show you? Read the letters, Ronnie. Perhaps they'll help to explain.'

Ronnie sat silently as his grandfather's frail voice drifted back into sleep, then he got up and went back to the table. Once more he put the briefcase beside him, and continued reading, allowing past and present to move step by step towards each other.

7

A PROBLEM FOR ISABELLA

LETTER TO MISS FLORRIE MAYNE
FROM MISS ISABELLA MAYNE
1 MARCH 1928 LONDON

Dearest Aunt Florrie,

It was lovely to get your letter.

Yes, I'm into my first term at St. Agnes' Training College and I'm really enjoying it. I wish my father would come and visit me, and see what good it is doing me. For the first time in my life I feel independent. I feel as though I have some say in my own life and am beholden to no one, except perhaps Phyllis Elliott herself, the Principal. It was only through her that I was able to gain a late entrance on to the course, though I was more than qualified and feel no guilt.

My only sadness is my father's hostility. Once it was clear that Henry was alive, my father wanted me to return home and wait dutifully until I am married.

I know he hoped that you would be able to influence me in this matter. Dear Aunt, I hope you do not feel offended and hurt that I decided to continue along the path I chose. I value your advice. I value the support you have given our family ever since Mother died. But you see, for me, it is not cut and dried. I have to rethink my life and my attitudes. I have to rethink Henry. I know from his letter that he is a profoundly changed man. India has changed him and for the moment he has become a stranger to me. I once loved a Henry Saville but is this the same man, who is at this very moment on the high seas returning home to marry me?

There is something I must tell you in confidence and beseech you not to tell my father or anyone else. I know I can trust you and I'm sure you will understand even more clearly why I felt impelled to continue my training and my bid to have the power to be independent. I do not think my father would be able to understand the situation. I feel he would be angry, turn against Henry – and I don't want that.

The fact is, Henry decided to adopt an Indian baby boy. He is bringing this boy back to England with him and he wants me to accept the boy as our child.

You will be shocked, I know. I have told no one else yet. I feel loath to be in the position of receiving mountains of advice or to have looks of pity thrown in my direction.

I am full of foreboding, I admit it. It would be different, perhaps, if we were living in India but that is not to be. Henry has been told that he will have one more year out there and then he is to work in the India Office in London. For my sake, I am pleased. I had not looked forward to a life in India, or to the prospect of our children being separated from us and being sent to boarding school here. But when I think of the future of the child. What then? Can we really bring up a child of alien blood and alien culture? Can we really bring him up to act and behave and be accepted as an Englishman? My common sense cries 'no!' And when we have our own? What then?

Oh, Aunt Florrie, I pour out my heart to you for you are the only one I can talk to and the only one I can trust. Why is Henry doing this?

You know most of the details of Henry's disappearance. What you and my father cannot comprehend is the deep bond that was created between Henry and the people in the forest who saved him. When they died of smallpox and the child was brought to him "to preserve his life as his was preserved", Henry felt a total sense of obligation and I feel from his letters, more than an obligation, a God-given trust. All I fear is the reality. The reality which in the end, this child, above all, must bear as he grows older and into manhood.

Henry's boat docks on the 26. Until I meet him, look into his face, know for sure that I love him, I cannot decide whether or not I can accept this adoption and this alien baby as our child.

I beg you, Aunt, support me. Give me your love. Pacify my father. His anger and hurt distress me beyond endurance.

Is there any chance of you coming to London? I have a spare bed in my room and could easily put you up. Please come if you can.

Your loving niece,
Isabella

My dearest Isabella,

Your letter shocked me indeed. I don't care what reasons Henry Saville puts forward, but that he should bring a native baby to England and expect you to mother it, is absolutely outrageous. I advise you to break off the engagement forthwith.

I have not broken your trust and told your father. As you say, he would be appalled. However, I want you to give me permission to tell him for I believe it is he who should meet Henry off the ship and inform him that you are no longer his fiancée. Please write to this effect by return.

Your devoted Aunt,
Florrie.

My dear Aunt,

I cannot do as you say. Forgive me. I loved Henry. He was the whole world to me. Until I meet him again, see and hear his story from his own lips and judge for myself, only then can I make a decision.

Remember, he is doing this from the highest and most Christian of ideals. He is a noble, good man and it is not for us to judge him yet.

I hoped for your sympathy and support. If you cannot extend these to me, then so be it. I must do what I think right.

I advise you not to tell my father or to let him meet Henry's boat for I shall be there and would not relish an unseemly scene on the docks.

Dear Aunt, should we not try to have some trust in a man who, up until now, we have admired for possessing the highest ideals of service to his country, honour and leadership?

Your ever loving niece,
Isabella

My dearest Isabella,

The baby was brought to me today from hospital. He is completely well and virtually unmarked by the smallpox, thank God. There is just a shallow pit on his brow and one on his left cheek, such as might be left after a bout of chicken-pox.

The ubiquitous Miss Murray from the mission came, too. Although I can't stand her pious superiority, I have to admit that she has organised expert help for me, having accepted, reluctantly, my decision to adopt this boy and bring him up as my own son.

I now have a wizened old ayah with barely two teeth left in her head but with the cunning of a crow and the cackle of a hyena. Old she may be but she is as agile as a goat, and she guards the baby with her life. Each day a young girl comes to help as well, also organised by Miss Murray. She's from the local orphanage and seems endlessly willing.

The doctor reminds me that the child needs a name, which confuses me. I hadn't even thought of it. Miss Murray assures me that I should have the child christened, which confuses me even more, remembering that he came from the hermit home of a very pious Hindu. I have decided on a simple but appropriate name, Manu. I felt there was a certain link to our Christian roots as Manu could well have been Noah, for like Noah, he was told by God to build an ark and save all living things from the impending deluge. Yes! Manu seemed to fit well for India. When I bring him to England is the time to think of a more suitable name for a boy who is to be brought up as an Englishman.

Meanwhile, I have discovered a use for the cooking pots. I somehow couldn't bring myself to relegate them to the kitchen. I find them so aesthetically pleasing to look at. I like the rounded, hand-wrought simplicity and the way they stand, the three of them, perfectly graded. I use them to calm me down at the end of a day and to prepare my mind for sleep.

These pots are far more intriguing than I could have ever imagined, and I learned about them from a most unlikely source – old Charlie, the dog catcher. Old Charlie, I wouldn't like to say how old, was born and bred in India. He's never been to England. Says he doesn't want to. He's a bit of a recluse which I suppose is not surprising since he doesn't have the most savoury of jobs. He has to tour the district on his bicycle all day long, with his rifle slung across his back, ready to shoot dead any stray dog which crosses his path. He lives alone, not quite in Civil Lines with the rest of the English community, and not quite in the bazaar with the Indians.

Anyway, to continue. I had the three pots out on the table on my verandah one morning and I was going to get the bearer to polish them up a bit, when old Charlie came by. We had called him into the compound to get rid of a wretched stray dog which had taken to hanging round the servants' quarters. It had to be killed. One can't take risks in India, not with rabies a constant hazard. When the job was done, I offered old Charlie a cup of tea. He pulled up a chair and glanced at the pots.

'What's these then?' he asked in his usual blunt fashion.

'They were left to me,' I replied, 'along with the baby.'

'Hmm! I heard about that,' says he. He looked at me closely. 'Reckoned you got guts, I did.'

'It was my duty,' was all I could say. 'But what do you make of these pots? I'm intrigued by them. The woman that brought them was old and dying of smallpox, and carrying a sick baby, and these pots aren't light, feel them! Why didn't she abandon them, or at least just bring one of them?'

Charlie leaned forward and looked at them hard. Then he lifted each one with as much care as he would a piece of china – not indifferently like most people. He lifted each pot and tested its weight in his hands. He ran his fingers round their bodies, feeling their shape and texture, then he put them back on the table leaving his hands enclosed round the largest one.

'Khumba!' he murmured.

'Khumba?' I repeated. 'What's that?'

'It's the Indian word for Aquarius, the Water Carrier. The pot is a symbol of so much – of life itself. The natives celebrate *Khumba* every year. When the sun enters the house of Aquarius, that is *Khumba* and they take their pots and walk, sometimes for days, until they reach a river. Then they immerse themselves in the sacred waters, fill their pots and walk home again. You see, when you think about it, the pots represent everything to do with Indian life. They are present at birth and death and marriage; at worship and celebrations. They are at every meal, at cooking, drinking, washing, cleansing – at almost every act of living.

53

'And you see,' Charlie held up a pot. 'Look at the round, seamless shape. It is a symbol of eternity, of the unbroken continuity of life within the universe. And it is not just the shape of the world. Watch the women on their way to the well. See how the shape of the pot responds to the human body. It rests in the crook of the arm, it sits on the head, it yields into the curve of the hip. Then look at its form as it stands in line with other pots. To look at a pot is to think of water. The well, the river, the meeting place, gossip at evening time round the water pump, and the winding pathways home through guava and mango groves. The pot is elemental . . . and yet . . .' Charlie paused.

I leaned forward utterly mesmerised and amazed by the poetry of his words. 'And yet what?' I whispered.

As if he hadn't heard me, Charlie caressed one of the pots with his finger. 'All pots are symbols. When one is broken or discarded, another must be created. Symbols cannot be abandoned. So there must be something more about these.' He ran his finger up the curve of the pot to the rim, and almost casually rubbed it round the rim, as I had done.

Immediately a low hum, like a voice from inside it, throbbed through his fingers.

It was as though he had received an electric shock. He recoiled, his face flushed with excitement. Then he placed the three pots in front of him in a row as if they were a musical instrument, and began to play them.

Each had a pitch of its own, and soon strange harmonies filled our ears. I joined in, and how we made those pots ring, till their pitches seemed to alter and trigger off other harmonics. Like two musicians we responded not just to the pots, but to each other, allowing our sounds to rise and fall like voices, blending in counterpoint.

Instinctively, our sounds reached a climax of such intense vibrations, that I felt as though my whole being had been invaded by sound. Then, simultaneously, we allowed the pitch to fall and fall, the throbbing harmonies to fade, until we were both left with a single pure note.

'It is like Lord Krishna's flute,' Charlie said, hardly audible. I stopped playing, and allowed Charlie's last note to hang in the air, dying away to silence.

For a while the silence itself seemed a part of the music we had just made. Neither of us broke it. Then a cry from the baby brought us back to reality, and Ram Singh's voice called uncertainly in the background, 'Sahib! Sahib!'

Charlie turned to me. 'I know the answer to your question now, Mr Saville,' he said, huskily. 'These pots are no ordinary cooking pots. They are sacred vessels. They are singing bowls!'

LETTER TO MISS FLORRIE MAYNE
FROM MISS ISABELLA MAYNE

Dearest Aunt,

Henry's boat docked on 26 March and I was there to meet him as promised. There was one other member of his family present, his sister Clare, whom I have met once before. His father, as you know, is dead, and his mother is in very fragile health and lives in Eastbourne.

I was relieved to find that Clare Saville was intensely practical. We had a short but valuable conversation in which she suggested that Henry and I spend a week or so in her house in Sussex where we could all try and come to terms with the situation.

She perfectly understood my need to be allowed to judge in my own time, and to decide whether or not I could marry Henry in these circumstances. She said if I could not, then she would invite Henry to live with her and she would bring up the child.

If I had any doubts about my love for Henry they were all swept away the moment I saw him coming down the gangway. Still, I had vowed in my own mind that I would not make any decision until we had had a few days together. I will forever bless Clare for enabling us to have this time. In a way, we started all over again, and just learned about each other as if from the beginning and it was even more perfect than the first time we courted.

Now for the baby. At first I could feel nothing for him except curiosity. He is a beautiful child, and anyone would feel bound to admire him. But it was only when over the next few days I heard Henry's story from his own lips, saw the tender way in which he loved and cared for the little creature that I found myself drawn closer and closer to it. I call him "Adam", though Henry says he must also have the Indian name "Manu" as a mark of respect to his parents. But if I were to be its mother I needed to call it by a more familiar name.

One day, Henry was out and Clare was gardening, so I was alone in the house with the baby. Suddenly it awoke from its sleep and began to cry. Until then I had always left it to Henry or Clare to attend to it but this time I was the one to hand. I held back at first, tempted to go down the garden and call for Clare, when I caught his eye. He stopped crying and looked up at me so directly, with so gripping a stare that I could not go. Instead, I leaned over and stroked his shining black hair. He reached up both his arms and I lifted him into mine.

In that moment I felt a surge of love. It was the sort of feeling I knew I would have were it my own baby. It was the sign I had been looking for. For the next few minutes we just got to know each other. He pulled my hair, and chewed my cheeks and gurgled and bounced and all the time, the happiness inside me was growing and growing. Then I laid him back down in his cot. Nearby were the three Indian metal bowls which Henry brought with the baby from India. He said that they were the baby's, and must never be parted from him. Henry rubs his finger round the rims and they make the most beautiful humming sounds. They never fail to calm the baby, and help him to sleep. For the first time, I tried it, too. Wonderful resonances throbbed from the metal. I have never been to the East, yet I felt it invoked all the mysteries and beauties that I had ever heard of, the magic that people from the West must somehow discover before they learn to love India. Henry discovered it, and now, though I will probably never go, I feel I have been there. I knew now that my love for Henry was quite quite big enough to absorb everything that he loved and wanted. This was our child. I was ready to be his mother.

So my dear Aunt, I told Henry that if he still felt that I was the wife that he wanted I was ready to be both a wife to him and a mother to the child.

I cannot describe the happiness we feel. I want you to share it, dear Aunt.

We have decided to marry in Sussex at St. Luke's Church on 27 April. We want it to be very quiet. Henry will only have his sister and his best friend Anthony, from his Oxford days. I would love to have you and, if only he could soften his attitude, my father. Can't you persuade him?

We have decided to have a brief honeymoon in Italy. Clare will look after the baby. We will then only have three weeks left before Henry has to return to India and complete his posting. Sadly, we have decided that I should stay in England with the baby and live with Clare. Having been so delicate throughout my life, Henry doesn't want to risk my health out in India, and it will be only for a year.

I know you have still not reconciled yourself to my actions and that you still feel I should have given Henry up. Come and see us. Come to our wedding, then I am sure you will be persuaded that our marriage was made in Heaven.

I love you, Aunt Florrie, and until I know I have your blessing, I shall feel a great loss deep inside.

Come and be a witness to my happiness.

Your ever loving niece,

Isabella.

8

WHERE ARE THE SINGING BOWLS?

'GRANDPA! The bowls! What happened to the singing bowls?' Ronnie spun round from the table. He couldn't even see his grandfather's bed now, so deep was the darkness which had invaded the room.

Roughly, Ronnie pulled round the table lamp sending its fringed, yellow glow tossing across the floor.

In the gloomy light, his grandfather's bed seemed to bob like a raft among the wildly swinging shadows.

He lay with his head turned upwards. His eyes were wide open, but glazed and fixed on some invisible point on the ceiling.

'Do you hear me, Grandpa?' Ronnie shook his arm. He no longer cared if he woke the old man. Now was no time for sleeping. Soon he would have the sleep of eternity, but before then, he must know more.

'The singing bowls, Grandpa! The baby, Manu, my father was never to be parted from them. That's what you said in your letters. I've never seen them. Where are they?'

'The singing bowls. Yes!' The old man gave a long drawn-out sigh. 'Yes, you'll need those, Ronnie.'

'But where are they?' Ronnie almost shouted.

'With the briefcase. Must be. Up on the wardrobe. I haven't looked at them for years.' His voice seemed to be rambling. 'I've always kept them near me. Never far away. You'll need the bowls, Ronnie. They should be yours now . . .' His voice faded away and he was asleep again.

Once more Ronnie stood in front of the wardrobe. The table lamp had stopped bobbing, and he found himself staring at his own image in the full-length wardrobe mirror. He was confronted by a thin, angular, olive-skinned youth, who frowned back at him with dark, disturbed eyes. He almost felt he saw three generations reflected before him, his Indian grandfather, his father and himself.

'Who am I?' Ronnie said out loud. 'Who might I have been in another country? Who could I choose to be?' For suddenly, he had the strange feeling that he was about to be presented with choice.

He pushed the chair closer and stood up on it, reaching into the dusty depths on top of the wardrobe. This time he was systematic. He swept his hand across from one side to the other, blindly identifying bundles of newspapers, magazines, carrier bags stuffed with more carrier bags, childhood toys which his mother hadn't brought herself to throw out, and just bundles of old curtains and bedspreads stored and forgotten. But he felt nothing which was solid enough or bulky enough to be three metal pots.

He climbed down, scowling with disappointment. 'Grandfather!' He addressed the slumbering form. No, it was no use waking him again. He must have forgotten where he had put them. Yet, if he was never far from them, then surely they must be somewhere in this room? He began to search. Behind the wardrobe, inside the wardrobe, under the bed – he looked in all the obvious places. But nothing.

He looked around again, to see if there was anywhere he had missed. His grandfather's room was a generous size but cluttered with objects of a lifetime. One wall was entirely covered by books, another held a large Indian painting; large in size, but miniature in style, it was so crammed with the detail of an Indian Maharajah's court. Brass elephants trooped across the hearth, cranes made from grey buffalo horn posed on one foot with long pointed bills and the curtains, cushion covers, table cloths and bedspread were Indian materials, leaping with colour and design.

At the foot of his grandfather's bed, Ronnie glanced at the long, low object he had always taken for a table, it was draped with an Indian embroidered shawl on which stood a solid stone statue of Lord Krishna. He stood in classical dancing pose, with his hands elegantly clasping a horizontal flute to his lips. Suddenly curious, Ronnie lifted a lower corner of the shawl. This was no table. There were no legs. Excitedly he lifted the stone statue away, folded back the shawl and found himself looking at a wooden, heavily carved chest with brass fastenings. There was no lock.

He lifted the lid. It was heavy. He looked inside, prepared for disappointment. Faded clumps of material had been tossed carelessly on top. He threw them out on to the floor, and then gasped. He had found them. Glowing in the darkness, he distinguished the sharp, metallic rims of metal pots.

He touched them tentatively, almost as if they would burn his fingers. He lifted one out, then another which was larger, and then . . . he felt around. That was all. There were only two bowls and another bundle of letters written in a hand he didn't recognise.

'Are you there, Ronnie?' His grandfather's voice called him feebly.

'There's a bowl missing, Grandpa!' cried Ronnie. 'There should be three, shouldn't there?'

'You've found them then?' the old voice quavered with relief.

'Yes, but only two bowls, Grandpa. Where's the third? Did you put it somewhere else?'

60

The old man was silent. Ronnie ran over to the bed. There seemed hardly anything left of the wasted body. His skin covered his bones so tautly and thinly that Ronnie felt he could almost see his skull underneath. His eyes stared out blankly, unseeing. He lay so still Ronnie panicked. 'Grandpa!' He shook him fiercely. The eyelids fell slowly and opened again. 'Two bowls!' he repeated as if in a dream.

Suddenly a tremor rang through his thin frame. Burning spots appeared on each cheek, his eyes came alive, glistening. He struggled to sit up.

'Of course! What a dunderhead I've been! Now it all makes sense. He must have played them, received a message from them, a calling. But he only took one pot. He left the rest, for you, Ronnie. He must have left the other two for you. Yes! The singing bowls will lead you to each other.'

The old man was almost springing from the bed with agitation.

'Bring them over here, boy. Let me see them. Let me touch them.'

Rapidly, Ronnie brought the two bowls over and placed them on the counterpane. The old man put a hand on each one and hugged them to him.

'Now I know he's alive. Now I know he was not running away from me or you or your mother. He was looking for home. He has gone home.'

'Do you mean my father?' whispered Ronnie.

The old man began to run his fingers round the rims of the pots.

'You will find him in the forest. You must go to him, Ronnie. Go. He will be waiting for you. Take the bowls and find him!'

The old man sank back exhausted into his pillows. Very gently, Ronnie removed the old man's thin fingers from the bowls. He sat down on the edge of the bed and held the bony, knuckled hands in his own.

He knew there was no one in the world he loved as much as his dying grandfather. He bent over and kissed his forehead. 'Thank you,' he whispered. Then he carried the two bowls over to the table in the window, and like a musician, sat down to play them.

9

LETTERS TO MY SON

12 NOVEMBER 1974

My beloved son, Ronnie,

A few hours ago, you were born. I held your small body in my arms while you were still moist and the cord which has fastened you to your mother all these months was still uncut.

How I love your mother Linda. She knew what you meant to me at that moment of birth. Even before she held you herself, she asked the nurse to give you to me, for she understood that I, who had been adopted; who had been separated at babyhood from all kith and kin and even country, had a special, overpowering need to hold you. You see, you are the first person of my own flesh and blood that I have ever known. Seeing you born, was like being reborn myself, and with you, I am going to grow up all over again.

As I held you, just a little while ago, your dark blue, new-born eyes were wide open. You hardly cried. You turned your head and looked around as if appraising us, taking note of the kind of world you had been born into, and thinking, 'Ah! So this is my mother, and this my father.'

As I gazed upon you, I remembered that my Hindu grandfather would have believed in reincarnation. Looking at you, with your Indian skin, and your thick black hair, I could almost have fancied that my mother or father had been reincarnated in you; that it was the only way they could come and share a life with me and love me through a lifetime which had previously been denied to us.

I write to you, my son, because even though you are but a few hours old, I have an overpowering desire to communicate with you, and through you, with my ancestors.

For the moment, I will write no further. This is a time of celebration. The drums must be beating in Heaven, and flower petals sprinkling down through the air.

I thank God for you, and for your mother Linda. I swear to try and bring you up with all the love and devotion of a father whose only desire is to bring you happiness.

Thank you for being born.

Your ever loving father,

Adam

Ronnie, sitting in his lonely circle of light, wept. Why? Why? The question stormed through his brain.

Why if his father had loved him so much, sworn to give him all his love and devotion, why did he leave them? How could he deprive his own son of a father as he had been deprived?

'Why, Grandpa?' he cried out into the darkness. But there was no answer.

Reluctantly, Ronnie took up the second envelope. It was far bigger and bulkier than the first and addressed to him.

He knew that the answer could lie within its pages. He was suddenly afraid.

LETTER FROM ADAM MANU SAVILLE TO HIS SON, RONNIE
16 APRIL 1980

My dearest Ronnie,

I am driven to write this letter, though God knows if and when you will ever read it. This may seem an unreliable way to communicate with my son, but it is the only way. If you never find this letter then perhaps it is for the best, for you may only despise me for my rambling attempts to explain my actions.

If you do find this letter then at least it means you have also found the singing bowls and I tell you this, Ronnie! Whatever failure I have proved as a father to you, there is nothing but good in the singing bowls and nothing but good will come out of your discovering their beauty and power.

I do not write to you as a child though at this moment you are only six years old. I write to you as an ageless being. Age has no meaning. Only understanding: that is all that counts.

Recently I have taken to playing the singing bowls in a desperate attempt to halt my growing state of uncertainty and confusion. Why, when I have a wife I love, and child who is my own flesh and blood, do I have a crisis of identity? I am in trouble and in conflict with myself and as I play the bowls and the strange harmonies throb through my brain and race through my bloodstream, the message comes through to me stronger and stronger. I must return to India.

I have tried talking to your mother Linda, but she cannot understand why I should hanker for a country I have never known, and with which she feels I have no ties.

Each day the pull feels stronger and I have become a man tormented. Yet this I know. Before I lose all control over my actions, I must leave you some account of myself so that if we never meet again, you will at least know who I was and that I loved you. Something my own, real father could not do.

When I look back over my life, have I not everything to be grateful for? Perhaps Linda was right. My home, my roots are here. Yet . . .

I was adopted by Henry and Isabella Saville and no two people could have been more loving and devoted as parents. If I started out as a mere fulfilment of an obligation Henry Saville felt towards my mother and grandfather who saved his life, I am certain that their sense of obligation turned quickly to love, for I have not one single memory of ever feeling unloved by them. I was loved as their own flesh and blood and perhaps even more so when it became clear that they were unable to have children of their own.

Of course, at first I did not know I was adopted. People didn't discuss such things. It was only when I started prep school that the colour of my skin was pointed out to me and it was made forcibly clear that I could not possibly be the natural-born English child of my white parents.

I will remember that morning in the school showers for ever. We all stood there, naked and exposed. All these white, white bodies and then mine, dark as a shadow. Different. Alien.

'You foreign?' asked a boy.

'No, English,' I replied.

'Has anyone ever heard of a black Englishman?' enquired a scornful voice.

'Perhaps he's just dirty!'

'Try washing, Saville.'

And how I washed, Ronnie. I scrubbed and pummiced my skin until it was raw. But I was brown all the way through and then I knew. I was not my parents' child.

I felt betrayed. I was nothing but a joke; a sham. I was blinded with fury. I ran away but barely made it to the porter's lodge on the edge of the grounds.

'Why did you run away?' asked the headmaster.

'Because I am not my parents' child.' I replied. 'So I can't be Adam Saville either.'

'Oh! And who do you think you are, may I ask?' said the headmaster, hardly able to restrain a condescending smile.

What could I say?

'Come on, lad, speak up!'

'I don't know, sir,' I hung my head.

'You don't know, sir? Been on this earth for nine years and you don't know, sir?' He grabbed my by my collar and twisted it to see the name tag on the inside.

'Whose name is written here?'

'Adam Saville, sir,' I muttered.

'Adam Saville, is it? So are you a thief then. If you're not Adam Saville, what are you doing wearing his clothes? Did you steal them?'

'No, sir.'

'Whose are they then?' he bellowed.

'Mine, sir.'

'Mine, sir!' he repeated with an extra twist to my collar which half choked me.

'And what is your name, boy?'

'Adam, sir.'

'Adam, what?' he demanded.

'Adam Saville, sir.'

'Ah! So we just have little lapses of memory from time to time, do we, Adam Saville? I believe that is how I was introduced to you by your worthy parents. But since it seems we are prone to a little forgetfulness, you will write, "My name is Adam Saville" five hundred times before tomorrow morning. Understood?'

'Yes, sir.'

Then suddenly he drew me even closer to him and bent his great, red face close to mine.

'And don't you ever, ever show such ungratefulness again. Ingratitude!' he spoke the word in a Shakespearean voice. 'Ingratitude is a sin.'

The next day, after I had written my five hundred lines, I was called aside after chapel where the vicar said much the same thing to me as well.

'We Christians do not like ingratitude, Saville,' he intoned. 'Remember that if you are to be a good Christian and a good Englishman.'

Ingratitude. The word was meaningless to me. Had I been ungrateful? For what? All I knew was that I had been lied to. I was not the person I thought I was. My whole life had been a pretence. Henry and Isabella, the two people I had loved and trusted in the whole world, had pretended to me that I was their child. But I wasn't. They pretended that I was white. But I wasn't. They pretended that a good public school would make me as good as any Englishman. But it was all an illusion.

We were all taking part in a game and I was forced to obey the rules. 'We won't tell your mother and father about this little incident, will we?' the headmaster had said confidentially. 'We wouldn't want them to be hurt by your ingratitude, would we?'

So I never did tell Henry and Isabella that my eyes had been opened; the veil pulled cruelly back. Ingratitude. Gratitude. These were not words in my young vocabulary. I felt love. I felt cheated. I loved Henry and Isabella, but I would never again call them 'Mummy and Daddy'.

Isabella noticed immediately. 'I expect you think calling us "Mummy and Daddy" is too babyish for you now. Ah well! I couldn't help shedding a little tear to think of you growing up so fast,' she wrote in a letter to me soon after.

I now called them 'Mother and Father' though even that felt a lie. Yet I did love them and never could tell them the pain I suffered at school; the bullying, the name-calling, the sniggering. For their sake, I played the game.

I suppose it was because of the war. The long separations and the insecurity, but I was sixteen before I had the courage to talk to Henry about it.

I had gained courage in that time and planted the seeds of a determination that one day I would inhabit the world as the person I really was. That I would be an Indian not a sham Englishman.

I was home for the summer half-term. It's a day that will always be fixed in my mind. Henry and I stood alone together in our Sussex garden. The garden was Henry's pride and joy and even I, uninterested as I was, knew that his garden was a work of art. He hurried me down the slope to where the garden ran into the rough beneath pine trees and wild shrubs. Excitedly, he showed me his new corner of rhododendrons. The flower was already out, its round, deep pink or red flowers glowing like beacons.

'Look at my rhododenrons, Adam!' cried Henry proudly. 'I've grown a whole little copse of them here to remind me of India. Of course in India they aren't shrubs but trees. Tall, slim, elegant trees that grow in the hills of the Himalayas.'

'Were there rhododendrons where I came from?' I asked quietly.

My remark was a like a pistol shot. Henry froze in confusion. What thoughts raced through his mind? What regrets perhaps? You see, Ronnie, it may be hard to believe, but no one had ever mentioned where I came from before. Oh, Henry often talked about India – where he had been, what he had done, and all his hunting exploits, but they had never talked about me as a child of India, or of who my mother and father were. 'Er . . . er . . . no. No rhododendrons that I can recall,' he stammered. He got his secateurs and began clipping flowers to take indoors. He seemed dumbfounded, though I'm certain they both knew that I knew I was adopted. It was an open secret, an unspoken fact. I helped him out.

'What was it like? I mean, what was it like where I came from? I know a bit about India; I've looked things up in the library and we've touched on it in geography. Everyone expected me to know about it, but I didn't.'

Henry cleared his throat uncomfortably. 'I see.' He said at last. Then after a pause he broke out furiously, 'Well, why should you know anything about India? You're English, my boy, and don't you forget it. You're as good as any man.' He bristled defensively. 'No one's been getting at you, have they?' He looked at me with eyes full of anguish.

'No, no,' I lied. 'Nothing like that. It's just that things come up from time to time. After all, I don't look English, do I?' I met his eye, challenging him to deny it.

Henry took my arm. There were tears in his eyes. 'Did I do wrong?' he asked, amost to himself. 'People said I was mad to bring you out to England. They predicted nothing but trouble. Has it been trouble, Adam?' He was begging for reassurance. I couldn't answer him.

'I loved India,' he said passionately. 'I could have spent my whole life out there, but it would not have suited Isabella. But I couldn't leave you. Your mother had entrusted you to my care. She and your grandfather saved my life.' He turned and gripped both my hands in his. 'They were two of the finest people I have ever known. In some strange way, they influenced the very core of my being. I owed it to them to keep you with me as my son. Do you see?'

I did see. If part of me had died in the washrooms of my prep school then another part of me was born again, as Henry and I walked quietly round the garden and he told me as much of myself as he knew; and he told me about the singing bowls.

The sun was dropping behind the row of conifers at the bottom of the garden when Isabella came out looking for us. 'What are you two up to?' she asked. 'You've been out hours.'

'I think we should get out the singing bowls, Isabella,' said Henry quietly. Isabella looked startled, even a little frightened. She and Henry exchanged glances though I pretended not to see. Oh, Ronnie! So much of life is pretending. I'm trying to make you see how this pretending gradually became a torture for me. It seemed there was no end to it – ever – not at any rate, here in England.

What was Isabella afraid of? Was she afraid that the singing bowls would bring the whole facade of our lives tumbling down? Was she afraid that I would at last discover who I really was? Did she in one piercing moment glimpse into the future and understand, if only for a second, what these bowls could do to me?

Our walk back to the house was in silence. The silence of trepidation – impending knowledge. There must have been such a silence before Pandora opened the box or before Alexander cut the Gordian knot. It was with a certain ceremony that Isabella and I sat down at the large, dark oak table, while Henry went to his study. We didn't look at each other, she and I, but just waited, each locked into our own thoughts.

Henry came back carrying in his arms a bundle wrapped in faded, shabby Indian cloth. He placed it on the table, and slowly

69

unwrapped the folds. I remember my heart thudding as though it would leap out of my chest.

One, two, three. He lined them up before us in order of size.

'Touch them, Adam,' he ordered quietly.

I touched them, one after the other, just with one finger, tracing round the pitted uneven surface of a hand-beaten copper body. My finger became an explorer, feeling its way around a new terrain, feeling every bump and indentation of the substance. I drew them closer to me and enclosed my hands around their shapes.

'Your mother touched these pots. She held them in her hands, carried them on her hip, tucked them into her arms. Your father too, and grandfather and who knows who else before them in your family, have held, carried and meditated before these bowls. By touching these bowls, you are touching them. When you learn to play them, your mind will make contact with theirs, and you will be reunited with them.'

The table shook suddenly, as Isabella jerked away. 'Henry!' she gasped.

'He has to know, Isabella. We always knew that one day, he would have to know. Come.' He got up and gently put his arm around her and led her from the room. 'They are yours now, Adam. Guard them always, and pray God they bring you peace of mind.'

10

INTERRUPTION

'Oh, there you are!' His mother's shadow fell across the room like a long, black exclamation mark.

'We'd better see to him now.' She came in carrying a chamber pot.

Ronnie was sure she hadn't seen the bowls and the table scattered with letters and papers. Hurriedly he swung the direction of the light away from it, and angled the beam towards his grandfather.

The old man stirred, as the light penetrated his closed eyelids.

'Time to get you ready for bed, Henry,' Linda said in a brisk, nurse-like tone. 'Just help me heave him on to it, then get the washing things,' she told Ronnie.

'Come on, Grandpa,' Ronnie spoke with gentle affection, as he pulled back the bedclothes. The old man's body looked lifeless already, lying so shrivelled and inanimate. With such ease was Ronnie able to slide his arms under his back and lift him, while Linda slid the chamber pot underneath. Then she took over supporting him, while Ronnie went to the bathroom and brought in the washbowl, soap, flannel and towels.

By the time he came back, a faint whiff of urine filled the air. Ronnie was used to this now, and hardly wrinkled his nose. He put the bowl down on the floor and once again raised his grandfather so that Linda could remove the chamber pot and take it away.

'What have you found out?' The old man looked up at him with bright, inquisitive eyes. 'Are you beginning to understand?' He squeezed his hand impatiently as they heard Linda crossing the landing from the bathroom.

'One thing I know for sure, Grandpa,' whispered Ronnie. 'My dad really loved you. I'm going to find him, you know. I'm going to find him even if I have to walk all the way to India.'

Linda strode across the room. 'India, did you say?' she snapped. 'Oh, so it's you, Dad, putting ideas in Ronnie's head about going to India. I wish you wouldn't. It only unsettles the boy. He's supposed to be working for exams, you know.'

She thrust an arm round his shoulders and started wiping down his face and neck with a damp flannel.

'Hey, take it easy, Mum. You're being a bit rough,' protested Ronnie.

'It's all right, Ronnie,' chuckled Henry weakly. 'I'm not made of bone china, you know.'

Ronnie eased off the old man's pyjamas, and swiftly, Linda soaped and sponged down his whole body, and then towelled it dry.

Now there was a sweet, soapy smell around the bed instead of urine. 'That's better,' smiled Ronnie sliding the pyjamas back on again.

'You're a good lad, Ronnie,' murmured Henry gratefully. His head fell back on the pillows, and his chest heaved up and down, quickly, almost fluttering. His fingers clutched the air, groping for the edge of his sheet. He was exhausted now.

Ronnie methodically rearranged the bedclothes around his grandfather. First he pulled up the sheet, then the two blankets, folded the sheet over the top and tucked it all in. Linda took the bowl of dirty water away, and when she had left the room, Henry gripped Ronnie's hand. His mouth worked soundlessly. He was trying to speak, but couldn't find the breath. Ronnie leaned closer to him.

'What is it, Grandpa?'

'Go to India, Ronnie. Find him. Promise me you'll find him. Tell him I'm sorry. Tell him I, we, Isabella and I, we loved him.' He clutched the boy desperately.

Ronnie stroked his hand reassuringly. 'I will go. I promise,' he whispered. Henry clung on to his hand, squeezing it tightly, then he relaxed slowly, subsiding back into his pillows and into sleep. Ronnie went on stroking his hand until his breathing steadied to a regular pace.

'Is he asleep?' Linda hovered in the doorway. Ronnie nodded silently.

'Are you going to come downstairs now? There's a good film on television.' Linda sounded wistful, and Ronnie knew she wanted him to sit with her.

'I . . . er.' He hesitated, really only wanting to get back to his father's letter. Instinctively he glanced towards the table. She followed his eyes.

'You've done all your homework now, haven't you? You've been up here . . .' she halted. Ronnie heard her intake of breath. She had seen the two bowls gleaming in the darkness.

'What on earth . . . How . . . What the hell are you doing with those?' she suddenly exploded.

Ronnie was horrified and frightened by her reaction. Even in the dim light, he saw she had gone deathly pale, her fists clenched by her side, her eyes staring as if she had seen an apparition. 'Where did you get them?' she finally choked. 'What have you been up to?'

'Mum!' Ronnie's alarmed whisper swung her round to confront him accusingly.

'It's him, isn't it?' She rasped. 'He's been telling you things. Wheedling away your affections. Turning you against me!' She pointed furiously at the bed. 'I knew we shouldn't have come to live with him. He never thought much of me. He's probably

73

known all along where Adam is. He's let me suffer all these years – and all the time he had those bowls – those damned bowls which Adam would never have been parted from without good reason. Now he's got his claws into you.' Her voice rose.

'Ronnie!' Henry's voice called feebly from the corner. 'Ronnie?'

'Hush, Grandpa!' Ronnie stepped over to his bedside swiftly, and stroked his head soothingly. 'Everything's all right.'

He heard the sudden movement behind him, as Linda fled from the room.

He followed her downstairs. She had run into the living room, still clutching the towel and dirty linen for the laundry. She stood in the middle of the room crying furiously.

'Mum!' pleaded Ronnie. 'You've got it all wrong. You really have.'

'Oh, I have, have I!' she sneered. 'You've been plotting, you and him. How long have you known about the bowls? You must have known they were your father's – he would have told you that. But why didn't anyone tell me? Had I no right to know? When Adam disappeared I looked everywhere for those bowls. I knew how he treasured them. Of course, they were just another barrier between us. He used to get them out secretly to play them. Meditating, he called it. All I know is, it was another 'no go area' into which I was not allowed. But I searched everywhere for them. They might have had a clue – or a letter – something . . .' She stammered to a stop as tears flooded from her eyes and choked her in a flurry of towels and handkerchief and the edge of her sleeve. She flopped down on to the settee and cried uncontrollably into the cushions.

'Please don't, Mum,' pleaded Ronnie, helplessly. He wanted to go forward and touch her. He wanted to hug her and persuade her she was wrong. Instead, he went to the kitchen and made her a cup of tea.

When he returned, she had calmed down a bit and was dabbing her face, though tears still gathered in the corners of her eyes and rolled down her cheeks in ones and twos.

'Here!' Ronnie held out the cup of tea. She took it, her hand shaking a little as she brought the rim to her lips. When she had gulped down several hot mouthfuls, she looked up at him exhausted.

Ronnie sat down beside her. 'You've got it all wrong, Mum.' He started again, quietly trying to explain. 'There's no plot. No conspiracy. It was me. I've been asking Grandpa about Dad. I wanted to know more. No one else will talk to me about him.'

'How can you say that!' Linda protested with a fresh burst of tears. 'When have I ever not answered your questions? You don't ever come to me – always to him.'

'No one has talked about Dad, all these years,' insisted Ronnie vehemently. 'Not you, or Aunt Janice, or Uncle Bob. "He's been forgotten. Think of him as dead." That's what I was always told when I asked about him. So I stopped asking, and it was as though he never existed. Even Grandpa wouldn't talk until now. Now he's dying. You talk about a plot. Yes, there was a plot all right. A plot to stop me learning more about my dad. It's true, isn't it? You wouldn't let Grandpa talk about him either.'

'No, I wouldn't!' she agreed bitterly. 'Once I knew he wasn't dead. Hadn't had some accident or lost his memory. Once I knew he had deliberately walked out of our lives, walked out on me, you – his own flesh and blood, without even so much as a note on the mantelpiece, he ceased to exist for me. He didn't deserve to exist. I'd rather he had died. The pain wouldn't have been so bad. Instead, he condemned me to a life of not knowing – and do you know the worst thing that he did to me? He destroyed me. He made me valueless. I wasn't worth even a scrap of paper on which he could have written "goodbye". So that's why I never wanted to hear his name again. And why should you, either? His betrayal of you was the worst, the most unforgivable. Oh, he made so much of you at the time. "My own

75

flesh and blood!" he said. You – the only other person he knew in the world who had the same blood running through his veins. He almost took to writing poetry when you were born. But it was all a lie. He never loved you or me. He couldn't have, otherwise he could not have been so cruel.'

Her cheeks, which had been bloodless, flushed red again with bitterness.

'And now you suddenly pop up with the bowls – the singing bowls. It's ten years now, and he can still insult me.'

'Mum! You did get one letter from India, I remember it.' Ronnie frowned, trying to sweep back the years and recollect the yellow, flimsy envelope covered in stamps. 'Was it from Dad?'

'You remember that?' Linda asked quietly. It seemed to calm her down. She finished off the cup of tea, then got up and walked over to her writing desk. Without hesitation, she went to a drawer and pulled out the same yellow, grubby envelope all covered with stamps. 'Do you mean this?' she asked holding it out.

Ronnie took it without a word. He opened it. She didn't stop him. He unfolded a thin, cheap bit of exercise paper and read the spidery, thin, pencilled words.

"Truly, it is not because of the husband that the husband is loved, but because of Self.
And it is not because of the wife that the wife is loved, but because of Self.
And it is not because of the son that the son is loved, but because of Self.
When Self has been seen, when Self has been heard, when Self has been understood and when Self knows itself, then everything is known."   4.V.1. – 4.V.6.

Ronnie read it through two, three times. 'What does it mean? Did my father write this?'

Linda shrugged. 'Henry said he thought it was from the Vedas – they're Hindu scriptures or something. It could be Adam's hand. I'm not sure. Does it matter?' She leaned back into the cushions and closed her eyes. 'According to the Hindus, nothing matters, at least, that's what Adam used to say. Damn the Hindus, damn the singing bowls, and damn the day I met your father. It's brought nothing but misery. Damn him up there,' she jabbed her finger upwards. 'Damn him for bringing all this trouble on us. Just because of some silly, sentimental, wrong-headed belief that he owed an obligation to a couple of natives . . .'

'My great-grandfather and my grandmother,' Ronnie reminded her gently. Their eyes met and held.

'Yes,' said Linda finally.

'Yes.'

A strange stillness hung over the house. Linda and Ronnie stared at each other. Both were thinking of the singing bowls standing on the table upstairs, gleaming in the darkness.

'What are you going to do with them?' asked Linda.

'Learn to use them. You know, things may not be what they seem. The bowls may help.' Ronnie looked at his mother quizzically. 'I think we need to start again, don't you? Forget what we thought we knew, and start afresh. But let's start from at least one truth. Grandpa didn't know those bowls were here till I found them, to night. So don't blame him. No one's to blame. It just the way life worked out. Let's stop blaming, can we, Mum? Let's see if we can find out a bit more of the truth. I need to know. Grandpa understood that. That's why he gave me his briefcase of letters and papers. I'm in the middle of a letter from Dad.'

'From Adam, you mean?' Linda jerked sharply. Ronnie nodded. He hoped she wasn't going to start crying again, and accusing. But she didn't. She was too tired now. Her eyes were red and swollen with crying, her body hung limp with the draining of her emotions, but she couldn't resist a last bitter retort. 'Do what you like,' she murmured. 'I'm too tired to care. I'm going to bed.'

Without looking at him once, she wearily left the room.

'Goodnight, Mum,' called Ronnie. There was no answer.

11

THE DECISION

The bowls have become an obsession. Ever since I learned to play them, I am like one addicted. What strange chemistry is this? They are more than metal, shape, space and air. The sounds that rise from them swell and expand till they seep into my ears, eyes, nose, mouth; seep into my brain and circulate through my blood stream so that I feel completely overwhelmed and I do not know minutes from hours, sleep from trance or reality from fantasy.

This was not always the case. At first they were just a sentimental curiosity. A link with my mother and my Indian background. They sat in my room, only to be looked at by me in school holidays. But each time I touched them it was like tasting, seeing, hearing. It involved all the senses, and gradually I began to spend more and more time, discovering the rich sounds which I could conjure up from them just by running my finger round the rims.

When I went to university, I took them with me. From now on, I would never be parted from them. They dominated all thought and action. No decision-making was possible, until I had played the bowls. I sensed a certain danger. I knew I should try and weaken the hold they had over me. I even debated getting rid of them, for sometimes their power is so strong that I wake in the night and am impelled to play them as if commanded to release the harmonies imprisoned inside them. It is as if they can read my thoughts, for no sooner do I think about freeing myself of them, then my eye catches myself locked in their reflections. I see my image beaten into the metal, curving round into the grain, stretching up to the narrowed rim, and plunging down into the black depths inside. It is impossible to see the insides of the bowls – and I could fancy that they contain infinity; forever; a darkness without end.

Whatever hand hammered those bowls and fashioned their shapes, now it is the bowls who are the masters, and it is they who take me as raw metal, and hammer me to do their will.

Now, whatever I have done, it is as if the bowls have allowed me to do it. Even meeting Linda, and loving her, has been with the permission of the bowls.

I have tried to play them to her, to make her see their wonders, but she only laughs. To her, playing the bowls is no more than an idle pastime, as meaningless as playing the rims of wine glasses after a meal. Yet the bowls told me to love her and marry her. How, do you ask? By the music they produce. By the rich harmonies which create positive feelings or negative feelings. It is a language I have learned to master and obey. For they have never been wrong – at least not until now. They rejoiced with me when you were born. Oh, the sounds I produced on the night of your birth – it was as if the whole universe throbbed with cymbals, trumpets and drums.

Yet now they demand I leave you. They first told me that the night of your first birthday. Why, why? I railed against them. I hurled them away. Why should they ask me to leave the child I had created? I blocked my ears, and for six years ignored the commands. But now, oh my son, my son. The call is too strong. I can feel my grip on you weakening. They are dragging me away.

25 April 1978

I am leaving you, Ronnie. I have to go. It will not be forever – only until first I and then you, stop living this lie and seek out our true selves. I must go ahead first. I was not who I thought I was, and I have not yet found out who I am. Therefore, my son, till I discover my Self, you too will be a stranger to yourself. This is why I must leave you. To Linda I will be dead. There is no message I can leave her yet.

I know it's through the bowls that I will reach my destination. I will take only one and leave you the others. One day, they will speak to you, too, and you will follow me for the same reason.

The man, who I know will love and protect you, perhaps better than I, is Henry Saville. He will be as good a father to you as he was to me.

God bless you both.

Your loving father,

Manu.

Not Adam any longer. Manu. India had reclaimed him.

The letter fell from Ronnie's fingers. He was numb. His eyes were unseeing, his ears deaf. His mind was as emptied of thought as a well run dry. All his senses were suspended.

He wasn't aware of reaching out, of drawing the bowls towards him, of embracing their shape within his arms.

He wasn't aware of his fingers smoothing round the rims of the bowls. The contact of flesh on metal, of pulse on reverberating air.

A low note throbbed through the darkness. It seemed to come from a great distance. Slowly it increased in intensity, growing and growing as it added harmonies to itself. The table beneath them picked up the vibrations and added to the dimensions of the note. They shivered down the legs into the floorboards beneath Ronnie's feet; ran across the room and up into the bodies of the other furniture. Now the vase on the chest of drawers was shivering, and the mirror on the wall, and soon it seemed as if every object and surface was responding and adding to the harmonies, till the whole house was like the inside of a church organ, reverberating like waves pounding on the shore.

'Ronnie!' A voice called from a million miles away. 'Ronnie! My messenger! My messenger is coming!'

Still Ronnie's fingers flew round and round the rim.

It was only when his mother's voice screamed, 'Ronnie! For God's sake stop!' and she hurled the bowls from his grasp, that he awoke like a sleepwalker, wide-eyed with terror and trembling uncontrollably.

She switched on the main electric light. A yellow brightness hit their eyes violently. 'Why didn't you stop when he called you?' She shook his arm fiercely. 'Couldn't you hear him?'

Ronnie rose to his feet unsteadily and staggered the few dazed steps to his grandfather's bedside. Henry's hands were outstretched across the coverlet, his fingers extended as if desperately reaching out for something. His eyes were open, fixed into a frozen gaze.

'He said, "My messenger is coming,"' whispered Linda, aghast. 'What did he mean?'

Ronnie knelt down and gathered the still warm hands into his own. 'Death,' he answered. 'He meant Death. The singing bowls summoned his messenger and now he's taken away his soul. It's all my fault.'

All through the rest of the night, Ronnie held those hands wishing that his own life's blood could stem the warmth draining away from his beloved grandfather. There was so much more he wanted to ask, so much more he needed to know. But by the time dawn broke across the grey suburbs and the sodium lights had dimmed into daylight, Henry's hands had stiffened and grown cold.

12

FIRST IMPRESSIONS

'Bloody hell!' Mike ejaculated furiously. 'This is impossible.'

Linda touched his arm anxiously. Her face was pale with fatigue, but blotched with red patches on her cheeks and neck from the heat. Beads of sweat gathered above her lip, in the curve of her chin and in the hollow of her throat.

They were standing on a traffic island in the middle of a chaotic junction of roads in Old Delhi. The roads were swirling rivers of humanity, among which cars, taxis, bicycles, an infinite variety of motor scooters, buses and animals moved in peculiar chemistry with each other, like molecules making up one vast, living organism.

And it wasn't just the sight of it but the sound. It was one shattering cacophany of car horns, bicycle bells, revved-up engines and human cries, against a background of Indian film-music blaring out of a distorted P.A. system, obliterating any ability to think rationally or calmly.

Ronnie stood a little apart from his mother and her boy-friend. Dazed and dispirited, stunned by the confusion around him. Nothing in Henry's letters and papers had prepared him for this.

'We can't just stand here,' he heard his mother's voice trying to be practical and decisive. 'Look! There's a park over there or something. Let's go there and sort ourselves out.'

Mike nodded curtly. 'Come on, Ronnie! And for God's sake, stop dreaming and stay close.' He grabbed his arm and urged him to the edge of the island. There was no break in the flow. They would have to take their chances like everyone else and just step out into the crazy current. Ronnie pulled his arm away and struck out alone. Linda's voice carried like a gull's cry in the wind, 'Be careful, Ronnie!'

Once across the road, they drew close to each other again like bewildered survivors, touching each other for comfort.

'God, what a place!' muttered Mike vehemently. 'Come on! Let's get into some shade.' He strode ahead of them, his shoulders hunched with annoyance and looked for a suitable place for them to sit under one of the tall, thin awkward trees. He prodded about the patches of brown stubble that attempted to be grass, then flung his rucksack down as if to stake a claim.

It smelt. Everywhere smelt. 'The place is one big bloody lavatory,' fumed Mike. Linda and Ronnie flopped to the ground and rested their heads wearily on their rucksacks, too tired to respond.

'Good morning. How are you? Very well, thank you. Do you want we get a taxi?' came the cheery sing-song voices of a group of grinning street urchins.

'Scram. Get lost.Buzz off!' Mike turned on them furiously. They fell back, scattering and as undaunted as sparrows. 'Thieving little brats, I shouldn't wonder.'

Ronnie jerked upright, looking fiercely at Mike. His mouth opened to speak. Linda caught his eye in time and threw him a pleading look. 'Don't,' it said. 'Please, Ronnie, don't.'

Ronnie knew what she meant. Don't get upset. Don't quarrel with Mike. Mike was Mike. He couldn't bear disorder, mess, chaos. To him it meant stupidity and failure. India was no place for the Mikes of this world but Linda had begged him to come. It was her condition for agreeing to the India trip. He shrugged and turned his back on both of them.

If only Henry Saville could have come to India with them. Surely he would have made sense of all this? Ronnie thought sadly. He'd have come alone if he could but Linda wouldn't hear of it.

'You must be mad, if you think I'd let my sixteen-year-old son go halfway across the world alone on some wild goose chase.' She still considered looking for his father madness. She was probably terrified of finding him alive. It would complicate her plans for marrying Mike. Mike! What the hell did she see in Mike? 'Thank God,' Ronnie thought, 'I'm old enough for it barely to matter. Two years and I'll be shot of them.' He kicked the dry earth bitterly.

It was mid-afternoon. The sun blazed down relentlessly. They were too exhausted to plan anything, but lay back, their limbs slightly akimbo, trying to encourage any whiff of cool air to circulate around their bodies.

They had four hours to kill before getting the night train to Durgapur, if the four hours didn't kill them first. When they were planning their journey in England, they had thought, 'Four hours! Good! Give us a chance to see round Delhi.' But they hadn't bargained for the heat draining them of all energy; of being first hassled by taxi drivers; then driven all over town, then cheated, until finally Mike had thrown three hundred rupees at the man, and bundled Linda and Ronnie out of the taxi in the middle of Old Delhi.

'If I have to do that too often, we'll be skint before the week is out,' raged Mike.

Ronnie leaned his head back on his rucksack. He could feel the singing bowls digging hard into the nape of his neck as if to remind him why he was here.

Ronnie closed his eyes and drifted into a half sleep.

It had rained on the day of Henry's funeral. Tears and rain. It was all the same. All sorrow for Ronnie, blaming himself for playing the bowls and not realising their power. Yet, yet, there had been a calm look on Henry's face, almost a smile in death.

84

Perhaps the messenger had not been a terrifying figure. Perhaps Henry had held out his hands to him as a friend.

Ôm. The journey to India had all been arranged so quickly, his mind had barely had time to adjust. Like a flip of the coin, they had whirled upwards into the air, and come down again, landing was it on their heads or on their tails?

Ôm. The sound seemed to reach him from a great distance, and yet so close it could have been from the bowls beneath his head.

Ôm. It penetrated his confused thoughts and filled all the cavities of his mind with its low, dark throbbing.

Ôm. The sound was as pure as a shaft of light; stayed constant; paused, then started again.

Ôm. Ronnie opened his eyes, just to a slit. Without moving any other single part of his body, he made out his mother and Mike, lying above him to his right; at arm's length, fingers just touching; asleep; their bodies curved protectively round their belongings. Beyond the group of Mike, Linda and himself, an outer circle had formed around them as a focal point. Two young men and their bicycles had flopped down at a barely polite distance, to eat their lunch out of a metal container and only make the slightest pretence at not being in the least interested in this foreign trio. At a similar distance from them, a half-starved dog slumped on his bony haunches, his body almost devoid of life. All that was left of his energies glowed in his eyes, fixed on the food, being rolled and manipulated by lazily, expert fingers and ejected into the mouths of the young men. Beyond the dog, a crow. Large, shining black and scavenging. He would collect whatever the dog failed to eat, as would all the dusty sparrows hopping about on the outer perimeter of the circle.

When he slid his eyes to the left, Ronnie could see the same street urchins tumbling and playing; yet like the dog and the crow and the sparrows, watching for the slightest movement. Forming part of the circle on the other side, squatted an elderly man in waistcoat and dhoti; he was going through the slow meticulous motions of preparing himself some paan. He set before him a row of little metal boxes. From the largest of these, he extricated a dark, green leaf which lay across the length of his palm. Deftly, he took a pinch of spices and betel-nut from each little box and spread them on to the leaf. Then he rolled the leaf and folded in the ends until it was exactly the right size for containing in the mouth. He paused, as if to increase the sense of anticipation; to set the taste buds salivating; then, fixing his eyes on the central group of people, he popped the package into his mouth and began slowly chewing, in circular, bovine motions.

Óm. Still the sound persisted, and at last Ronnie sat up with wide-open eyes to look around him.

A perceptible quiver ran through the onlookers as Ronnie took in each one of them. When he got to his feet the young men stopped eating, the children stopped playing, the paan-eater stopped chewing. The crow cocked his head and stared at Ronnie with a hard, dead eye, and the dog cringed, as if preparing himself for a blow. But Ronnie ignored them all. His attention was fixed on a figure sitting beneath a tree about fifty metres away.

Óm. Ronnie knew the sound came from him. He moved towards it as if drawn by a thread.

The group fluttered; unsure of itself. Follow him? Or stay concentrated on Mike and Linda still sleeping? It was the children who broke away from the circle to follow Ronnie, while the young men, the paan-eater and the animals shrugged, as if to say, 'This is where the focal point is. The boy will be back.'

The man was naked, except for the wooden beads around his neck, the black string around his loins, and the pale grey ash which covered his whole body. He sat cross-legged, upright, his hands resting lightly on his knees, his eyes closed. He breathed in until his stomach became a great hollow, and his bony ribs expanded like the walls of a cave. When he breathed out, the sound came. Almost inaudibly at first, like a low, distant echo reverberating from the very bowels of the earth.

Ôm. Slowly, slowly, yet increasing in volume and intensity, the sound was expelled; on and on it pulsated, till Ronnie felt it was never-ending. But at last, the ribs contracted, the stomach refilled the cavity and the sound died away to nothing. He heard his grandfather's voice inside his head; 'to Hindus, Ronnie, the creation and destruction of the world is but the breathing in and the breathing out of Brahma, the God of All.'

What infinitesimal universe had been created and destroyed in those few moments? Ronnie wondered. He felt an urge to come with his singing bowls and sit before this holy man. He felt sure the language was the same.

'Oi! Ronnie!' Ronnie flinched. He didn't turn, but instead waited to see if the holy man had been affected by the alien sound of Mike's voice. But no reaction flickered across his still, grey face, so Ronnie stepped lightly backwards and reluctantly returned to the circle.

'Don't wander off like that,' grumbled Mike. 'What the hell were you doing anyway? You shouldn't go hanging round some of these weirdos. I've heard stories about them. Just stay close, will yer?'

'We're in India now, Mike,' retorted Ronnie. 'It's us who are the weirdos! He's normal.'

'Oh, I see! We're experts on the Oriental, are we?' sneered Mike.

'Oh, come off it you two,' Linda chided them sleepily. 'God, I feel awful.' She sat up, her face white beneath the perspiration which lay across the surface of her skin.

'We need a meal and drink!' announced Mike, giving Linda a worried look. 'I think we should get to the station. We're bound to find something there, and perhaps some decent bogs! I need the loo.'

At the first sign of movement, the urchins came dancing in with their sing-song voices. 'You need taxi?' the tallest of the boys challenged them with an enticing toothy grin. Everything about him seemed to stick out. He had sticky-out teeth and sticky-out ears and his elbows and knees and shoulder blades, all stuck out in bony angles as he stood poised to rush off if Mike gave the command.

'No, we don't need taxi!' Mike cried firmly.

'You need guide?' asked another. 'I show you very good places. Cheap souvenirs. I show you. Follow me?' He beckoned energetically with sparkling, persuasive eyes, and even Linda laughed.

'They never give up, do they!'

'Ignore them,' muttered Mike, 'otherwise we'll have them on our backs for the next two hours.'

'Do we know our way to the station?' asked Ronnie.

'Station? You want station?' chimed in the boy. 'I take you. You follow me.' He grabbed Ronnie's arms and tugged him. 'Come? Come?'

'We're going in a taxi,' asserted Mike.

'Taxi thirty rupees, fifty rupees. I show you station for five rupees. Not very far. You follow.' The boy began to gather up their rucksacks and looked as if he intended to carry them all.

'Hey, you!' Mike grabbed them back, and forced the child away. 'Get away, damn you!'

'I'd rather trust the boy than another taxi driver,' commented Linda wearily. 'Let's just follow him. We can always pick up a taxi if he's having us on.'

The urchins took that comment as an agreement. They sprang in and once more collected up the rucksacks, almost toppling under the weight, but insisting they could carry them.

'You do realise we're saddled with them all, don't you?' snorted Mike. He whirled on the boy who had made the offer. 'Five rupees for the lot of you. All.' He demonstrated with his hands.

'OK. OK,' beamed the boy, and set off, staggering in a drunken way, across the grass towards the main road.

The young men with their bicycles giggled confidentially, strapped their lunch tins to their bicycles, picked them up, and strolled casually along at the rear of the procession.

As the dog, the crow and the sparrows homed in on whatever crumbs were left in their train, the paan-eater remained in his squatting position gazing at the departing figures, then as if by way of a comment, spat a high arc of red betel-nut coloured saliva in front of him.

13

TOWARDS DURGAPUR

Perhaps only the kite, its wings outstretched, as it drifted imperiously high above the city, would have detected a straggle of a procession threading its way through the teeming bazaar towards the railway station. The urchins in front, like ladybirds with the red knapsacks on their backs, had found their rhythm and slowed down to a steady trot. Behind them, red-faced and panting, strode Mike, certain that every cow which meandered in front of him, or every specimen of humanity which lurched up against him was part of some kind of conspiracy to separate him from his belongings. Struggling to keep up with Mike was Linda, her face blank with fatigue, moving almost rigidly as if on a slowly unwinding spring. Bringing up the rear, some metres behind, was Ronnie. He walked deliberately apart with a studied casualness, stopping to look at stalls, and allowing himself to be waylaid by street-sellers.

'Keep up, Ronnie!' Linda wailed, panicked at the thought of losing him. 'We must stay together.'

'Stop worrying, Mum,' Ronnie shouted back in irritation. 'I'm here.'

Suddenly they could see the incongruous Victorian Gothic spires of the railway station rising above the grubby shacks and buildings of the old city.

They had hardly dared to acknowledge the intensity of the heat outside until they stumbled into the ticket hall, and though there seemed no corner of the city, inside or out, where the population didn't flow, they each found a space to fall thankfully to the ground and press themselves against the cool stone.

The boys dumped the rucksacks unceremoniously and stood expectantly, their bony chests heaving with the exertion, their black eyes bright with triumph for having got them there.

Mike dug gracelessly into his pocket for the five rupees he'd agreed to pay them.

When they had pocketed the money, the eldest boy said, 'Which platform? What is your destintion?'

'Don't they ever give up?' snorted Mike. 'Clear off, now. I can find out the platform.' He turned to Linda and Ronnie. 'You two stay here and guard the rucksacks while I go and check our reservations and find the platform.'

'Yes, sir!' Ronnie saluted sarcastically, resenting the way Mike always handed out orders.

'Got a better plan?' Mike snarled back. 'Want to take over?'

'Oh, stop it, you two,' pleaded Linda. 'Of course he doesn't, Mike. Take no notice. It's the heat. It's getting us all down.'

'Huh!' Mike grunted, and marched off towards the Information Desk, somehow managing to keep an arrogantly straight line even if it meant stepping over bodies, or elbowing his way through groups of people. The eldest urchin ran alongside him like a persistent shadow. 'I show you office,' he chanted. 'I take. You see.'

'God, I feel awful!' Now that Mike had gone, Linda seemed to flop like a rag doll. She heaved herself up against her rucksack and put her arms round it as if for comfort.

'You OK?' Ronnie asked anxiously.

'I wish you and Mike wouldn't fight all the time,' she sighed weakly. 'Why do you provoke him so much?'

'Sorry, Mum. It's just that . . . well, he gets up my nose. He's so bloody bossy. Treats us all like kids. Treats you like a kid. I wish he hadn't come. We'd have done much better on our own. He must be hating it – I mean – it's a bit much coming out to look for his girlfriend's husband, isn't it?'

'I haven't a husband. Not any more. We're here for your sake, and don't you forget it. I'd go home tomorrow if I could. God, I feel awful!' She dropped her head on to her arms with a moan, and Ronnie felt a momentary unease. Though he would never admit it, he, too, would have given anything to be back home in England. Once again, they were the centre of attraction, ringed by expressionless Indians, just staring, staring, so that Ronnie wanted to jump up and shout at them, pull faces, give them something to stare at, stick out his tongue, wriggle his ears – anything. As it was, he turned inwards towards Linda and studiously avoided their eye contact, waiting for Mike to return.

He was away a very long time, and when, finally, Ronnie picked out his tall figure wending his way back, he seemed a little less arrogant than before, and once again, it was the triumphant urchin who led the way, and Mike who followed.

'I thought everyone was supposed to speak English in this damned country,' complained Mike as he approached. 'It's like trying to get blood out of a stone just finding out which platform we go to. Anyhow – it's platform eight. Come on!'

He made as if to pick up the rucksacks, but once more the urchin and all his mates who had never really gone away, ran forward and seized them possessively. 'Platform eight?' sang the urchins. 'We know. You follow!' they instructed, and off they went once more with Mike, Linda and Ronnie following meekly behind.

Platform eight writhed with bodies. The urchins thrust their way through and created an area near a food stall.

'Why can't we go to a waiting-room?' protested Linda, but none of them had the energy to move again, so they flopped down miserably on to their rucksacks to await the train.

Linda sat with her back rigidly against her rucksack, her head bent into her hands. Night fell with the rapidity of a stage curtain, yet the play was not over. The drama continued under the dull, yellow light of weak-powered electricity, and the feeble, flickering glow of the kerosene lamp.

Every bit of the platform was taken up and possessed; with bodies endeavouring to sleep like prone corpses beneath filthy winding sheets; by gaunt-faced families squatting in weary huddles sharing out cold chapattis and scoopfuls of dhal; travellers, hawkers, beggars, dogs, rats and cockroaches, each had their space on the platform, each their reason for being there.

Only Mike, pacing up and down, looked alien and out of place.

'Bloody country!' he kept muttering. 'Should never have come.' He looked accusingly at Ronnie. 'It's all your fault,' his eyes implied.

The urchins who had brought them to the station still hung around. The oldest boy who had shadowed Mike, now attached himself to Ronnie. He examined him closely, copying every action he made like a mirror image, and grinning disarmingly every time he caught his eye.

'What is your name?' he demanded in a high, jagged accent.

'Ronnie,' replied Ronnie amiably.

'Ron-ee,' The boy repeated the name several times to familiarise his tongue with it, then he stabbed a finger to his chest and introduced himself. 'Deepak!' he announced proudly.

'Deepak!' repeated Ronnie. 'Hi, Deepak!'

Suddenly Linda groaned and retched. 'I'm going to be sick!' she gasped. Ronnie and Mike leapt to her side and hauled her bodily to the edge of the platform. Her body contorted with agony as she vomited violently on to the track. When it was over she fell back half fainting into Mike's arms.

'Are you fit to travel?' exclaimed Mike, looking panicked.

'What do you mean?' cried Ronnie, suspicious that Mike was on the look out for any excuse to cut short the journey. 'We're not missing this train!'

'For God's sake get the water bottle,' Mike rasped. 'Typical of you to care more about catching the flaming train than taking care of your mother.' Ronnie loathed him. He pulled a water bottle out of his rucksack. There wasn't much left in it, and that was warm, but Mike snatched it from him and made Linda drink it all.

'Got to keep up the fluids,' he urged knowledgeably.

Linda immediately retched again. 'Oh God, I think I'm going to die,' she wept.

'Perhaps we ought to call it a day right now,' suggested Mike. 'Stick round Delhi. At least it's civilisation, and when you're better, we could see some sights and then go home. You're not fit for a wild-goose chase.'

'How can you say that?' cried Ronnie furiously. 'We can't give up already. To you, this is just a wild-goose chase. Well, you go home. I'm here to find my dad. Don't listen to him, Mum. You've got Delhi Belly. Everyone gets it. You'll be all right in a day or two if you take those pills the doctor gave us.'

Mike's reply was drowned in a shrieking of whistles, and a deafening blare of the siren as a diesel engine of monstrous size ground its way slowly into the station. It pulled behind it a long snaky train of carriages from which protruded a veritable forest of outstretched arms and heads and bodies leaning out of windows and half-falling out of doorways swinging open. Around them, the platform seethed into life with a great choir of voices, as if some invisible conductor had waved them in with a baton.

94

Ronnie clutched as many of their possessions as possible and at the same time tried to shield his mother protectively as a tidal wave of people poured on and off the train.

Mike and Deepak pushed their way along, looking for their reserved seats. 'I'll come back and get you,' yelled Mike. 'Just stay put.'

Linda moaned. Ronnie heard her, despite the roar, and suddenly he was afraid. What if Mike were right? What if Linda really was too ill to carry on? He encircled her with an arm. 'You, OK? Mum? We'll soon be out of this.'

He heard his name piercing over the top of the cacophony like a high piccolo. 'Ron-ee, Ron-ee!' Deepak appeared with two of his pals. 'You come now. Follow me.' The boys scooped up the rucksacks and Ronnie lifted Linda to her feet, keeping his arm round her so that she could lean on him.

'Deepak,' he pleaded. 'Don't go too fast!' as Deepak slid into the crowd like a snake. Deepak dropped back grinning and let the other boys sidle on ahead.

'Don't worry, Ron-ee. You OK. This your train.'

Deepak led them to a second-class compartment. It seemed crammed with people. Ronnie wondered where their reserved seats were. Mike was furiously gesticulating with someone, and managed to move a man, his wife and two young children out of the carriage.

'Bloomin' nerve. Took our reserved seats,' he muttered as they pushed their way into the compartment. He took out a sleeping bag and unrolled it on to the hard wooden slats of the seat.

'Here, Linda. Lie down and stay put, otherwise some other blighters will come and pinch your spot. You too, Ronnie. You get on top.' He indicated what Ronnie would have taken to be the luggage rack.

'What me, up there?' he gasped.

'Yeah!' For the first time Mike laughed dryly. 'It's a two-cum-three berth,' as they call it. This middle bit here,' he pointed to what was the back of the seat. 'This pulls out and becomes another bunk. It's all ours. We reserved it.' With everyone now in their rightful place, there was a sudden lull. The other passengers looked smugly at each other and were all ready to set up an atmosphere of camaraderie to see them through the long hours ahead. Mike went off to stock up with bottles of pop, the only safe thing to drink now that the sterilised water in their water flasks had run out.

Deepak looked at Linda lying outstretched on the seat, her face ashen.

'She friend?' he asked Ronnie.

'My mother,' said Ronnie.

Deepak frowned. 'Mother?' He noted the different colour of their skins. 'And Mike?' He looked puzzled. 'Mike father?'

'No,' laughed Ronnie. 'Mike friend. Her friend,' he added disassociating himself.

Deepak nodded as if in understanding. 'Where your father?' he persisted.

'Here. In India,' said Ronnie. 'We are looking for him.'

'Father Indian?' asked Deepak.

'Yeah!' said Ronnie shortly.

'Good,' smiled Deepak. 'Then you Indian too. If mother ill, she stay with friend. You come with me to find father.' He put his hand on one side engagingly.

'Oh no! I can't do that!' laughed Ronnie. Yet. He glanced at Deepak as if a door had been opened on a new possibility. Their eyes met, then Ronnie looked away almost embarrassed, wondering which of the two of them was the more mature and wordly wise. Though at sixteen, he towered above Deepak, a puny boy of not more than twelve years old Deepak made Ronnie feel the younger.

The train siren blared a warning. The urchins made no move to leave, but crouched in the corridor outside. Mike came bustling back with an armful of bottles of pop. He glanced in irritation at the boys. 'Are they still here?' he asked.

'Have you given them something?' suggested Ronnie.

'I suppose they deserve another two or three rupees,' agreed Mike grudgingly. He plonked down the bottles and fiddled in his pocket for some coins which he handed to Deepak without counting.

Ronnie wondered if they wouldn't have preferred a bottle of pop.

'I hope you gave enough,' murmured Ronnie. 'We couldn't have done without them.'

'Course we could,' grunted Mike. 'You're too soft.' He waved a hand at them, indicating that they should now leave the train.

The train was pulling away slowly, slowly, bit by bit as the boys tumbled out on to the platform. Deepak stood a little apart from the rest. Ronnie thrust a hand into his pocket. It closed on a note – he didn't know for how much. Without examining it, he reached out of the window and pressed it into Deepak's hands.

The look on Deepak's face spoke of more than just gratitude. There was already a bond between them, and now it was sealed. He tipped his head on one side. 'Hope you find father.'

Ronnie stayed at the window a long time after the train had left the station. It gathered speed through the suburbs and headed for the open countryside.

14
ED McGILL

Night trains. Night terrors. It was new to Ronnie. He lay on his cramped upper bunk fighting a sense of terror which threatened to overwhelm him. The train had been going some hours now, hurtling through the night, the carriage rattling and swaying as the wheels pounded blindly along the rails. Ronnie thought about crashing. He imagined the train leaping the tracks, rocketing through space, and in that second of free flight a thousand voices screaming their last human sound before being smashed to oblivion.

The train seemed to be going even faster. Its wheels echoed and changed pitch as they thundered over bridges and ditches; clickety-click, clickety-click, clackety-clack, clickety-clack, clackety-clack, clackety-clack. He heard its chattering sound multiplied like clapping hands reverberating through wayside groves and copses.

Below him, Linda moaned. Another wave of fear overwhelmed him. What if Linda were really ill? What if she died? It would all be his fault. He could see Mike's accusing eyes.

Night trains; night fears. Now the full shock of India hit him. Until now, they had simply concentrated on surviving their first day; getting from the airport to the city; getting around the city, finding where to eat, what to drink and how to get to the station to catch the train to Durgapur. It was obvious that they must start the search in Durgapur, for that was where Henry Saville had been Assistant District Commissioner, and that was where Ronnie's father had been brought as a baby.

Lying in the darkness, the search was forgotten.

Only the shock of India made his senses reel. Ronnie felt he had lost himself out here, and lost control of his purpose. Perhaps Mike was right. They should never have come. How could they possibly find his father in all this turmoil?

He groaned out loud and shifted his position. One of the singing bowls in his rucksack dug into the nape of his neck. He rolled over in the darkness to reposition the rucksack to make a more comfortable pillow, and his hands closed over the hard, round metal shape.

'Oh, Grandpa!' he whispered with a sudden surge of grief, and he bowed his head on to the bowl.

Even through the tough covering between his brow and the bowl, he felt a kind of throbbing as if it were alive. A strange tingling pulsated through his head. Gradually his panic subsided. The rhythm of the train merged with his breathing.

The train whistled a long, high triumphant note which rose a full tone and ended with a flourish. It seemed to defy the demons of the night. The train was slowing down. Ronnie felt the rhythm of the wheels relaxing.

The train had come into a station. No one in the compartment stirred. Only Mike uttered something about 'Don't they know we're trying to sleep?' and tucked his head even deeper into his sleeping bag.

Wide awake, and intensely curious, Ronnie crept from the compartment into the corridor. The train door was already swinging open, and a tea seller was calling inside, '*Garam Chai.*' Hot tea! The voices of other sellers and hawkers overlapped as trolleys piled high with fruit, sweets, pooris and cakes were pushed up the platform. There was no deference to the night or the sleeping passengers, and soon more and more people tumbled, towsled and creased, off the train to stretch their legs or look for sustenance. Soon the platform was as crowded and as busy as a bazaar.

'How long are we stopping?' Ronnie asked the guard who appeared at his shoulder.

'Fifteen minutes!' he replied.

Ronnie felt bold enough to wander off down the platform a little. He began to enjoy the sense of being part of the crowd and to feel independent. He noticed passengers joining a cluster of people around a steaming trolley of huge, clattering kettles and simmering saucepans.

Arms stretched, waving for attention; voices demanded. With rhythmic rapidity, the vendor and his boy helper boiled and stirred, mixed and brewed, poured and ladled using dried woven leaves for plates, and small clay cups still hot from the potter's kiln round the corner, for tea. Purees were kneaded and rolled and tossed into boiling vats of oil. The smells invaded the station. Ronnie wanted it all. Made bold by hunger and thirst, he picked his way over sleeping bodies, and bundles of belongings to get to the trolley. He fingered the money in his pocket. It felt alien. He shuffled closer and closer till he made eye contact with the vendor, then pointed out his order. The rhythm never faltered, even when Ronnie extended his hand with a variety of coins, and nudging, friendly bystanders all participated in extracting what payment was owing. Soon, with a quiet feeling of success, he was retreating back through the crowd with a leaf plate of purees and curry and a cup of sweet, boiling tea.

Suddenly he was aware of a movement at his feet. A claw-like hand rose from what he had taken to be a bundle of rags. It reached out towards his leg. Instinctively, Ronnie recoiled in disgust. The bundle stirred again. Another wizened, scrawny arm reached upwards, pleadingly. Ronnie realised he was looking at two ancient people, an old, old man and an equally old woman. They lay side by side in their bed of rags. They had placed themselves strategically to be near the food trolley where they could appeal to those more affluent. Now they looked up at Ronnie with large, dark eyes which seemed to take up the whole of their shrivelled faces.

'Just give them some puree and curry and the rest of your tea. You can afford it, and they'll get a better night's sleep with something in their bellies.' A soft American voice spoke in his ear. He had appeared out of nowhere. How could Ronnie not have seen him coming? He was a giant of a man; as if plucked from a surf board in California, with his broad shoulders, bare, tanned arms and long, flowing blond hair gathered beneath a headscarf, he stood out in antithesis to everything around him. He was wearing torn, faded jeans and a filthy singlet and carried a red rucksack, much smaller than Ronnie's, slung over a shoulder, as casually as if he were off to the beach for the day.

His eyes were a hard blue, yet he grinned at Ronnie disarmingly. 'It is your duty, 'Dharma'. Then you will have performed the act of a good Hindu or a good Christian. Both say you should give to the poor if you want to achieve Nirvana.'

Ronnie was speechless. The American moved towards the food trolley. The crowd yielded to him as he stretched out a long arm. 'Give me tea, purees and dhal,' he said in Hindi. 'Enough for two.' He received it instantly and gave half to Ronnie.

'Go on! Give the old people yours. If it's your gift, you get the good mark up in Heaven.' He smiled sweetly.

Ronnie held out the leaf plate and the clay cup of tea to the old couple. Both were deftly snatched from his hands with grateful murmurs and nodding heads.

'Here!' The American gave Ronnie his own portion of food and drink. 'Now I give to you, and I get a good mark, though I don't suppose you are as needy as they are. Go on, eat. Like this.' He took a puree and scooped a dollop of dhal and curry into his mouth with it.

Ronnie copied. 'Mmm. It's good,' he spoke at last.

101

'The best!' agreed the American.

They ate in silence watching the ancient couple at their feet sharing every single morsel of food and every single drop of tea, before sinking back into their bed of rags and disappearing contentedly from sight.

The train whistle shrieked. Ronnie was startled. He had almost forgotten time and where he was. 'Heck! The train. It's going. I must get on!' He broke into a run. When he reached his carriage and grasping the rail climbed aboard, he realised that the American was right behind him.

'You coming too?' asked Ronnie, standing back to make room for him.

'Yup!' He clasped the rail and swung on to the train.

Like some alien, planetary outpost in space, the brightly-lit station, with all its lights and noise and population slid from sight, and the train broke free once more and sped on into the black night.

The two leaned on either side of the door looking at each other, their profiles mirrored in the night glass. Now that they were face to face, Ronnie saw that the American was older than he had first thought. Nearer thirty than twenty. He saw too, that despite the impression of strength and muscular power, his face, like his body, was bony and gaunt, sheared down to his large frame from months of backpacking, eating rough, sleeping rough and ravaged by the variety of illnesses that travellers in India are prey to. Red cold sores clustered round the corners of his mouth and round his nostrils, and those blue eyes at first so hard, now fluctuated and clouded over as if shadows passed over the surface.

In between smiles, his face was taut, almost mask-like, but now, he smiled like a genial beach boy and held out a hand. 'I guess we should introduce ourselves in good British tradition, I presume?' he teased.

'How did you know I was British?' frowned Ronnie.

'You British Indians stand out a mile,' grinned the American. 'And I bet I know more Hindi than you do. Here!' He grasped his hand. 'I'm Ed. Ed McGill.'

'Ronnie,' replied Ronnie warmly returning the pressure. 'Ronnie Saville.'

'Gee! Even the name's English. God! Was your dad English, then?'

'No, Indian.'

'Don't tell me his name was Ronnie Saville!' Ed grinned, but there was an interested glint in his eye.

'Adam.'

'Geeze! I keep meeting Indians with British names. The nicknames are the worst, Bunty and Dolly, Teddy and Corky! You'd think they'd stepped straight out of P. G. Wodehouse. What is it with you Indians?'

'My dad was adopted, that's why he has that name.' Ronnie was defensive. 'My grandfather, not my real one of course, my English one, he adopted my dad as a baby in India and brought him to England. He was brought up there, married my mum, who's English, had me, then . . .' he paused. Why should he go on? Tell a perfect stranger?

'Then?' drawled Ed McGill.

Ronnie shrugged. 'He came back to India.'

'Looking for home?'

'Maybe.'

'And you? You looking, maybe?'

Ronnie shrugged again.

'Sure, sure. Everyone who comes to India is looking.' Ed sighed and drew himself up. 'And I'm going to look for a rack to stretch myself out on. Where are you getting off?'

'Durgapur.'

'That's four hours on. You can get some sleep. See yah around, pal. Maybe!' He winked, then lurched off down the corridor towards the front of the train.

Ronnie watched him till he'd turned the corner into the next carriage, then crept back into the darkened compartment. As he passed Linda's sleeping head, he knelt down and listened to her breathing. It was steady. He kissed her lightly on the forehead as she used to do to him when he was a child. 'The lip test,' she called it. 'The surest way to check a temperature.' Her forehead was cool, though damp with perspiration. It was hot. Very hot. The fans whirring in each corner of the compartment only churned the hot air round and round.

He climbed back into his luggage rack, carefully avoiding any contact with Mike whose body overhung every side of his bunk, and fell deeply asleep.

15
SEARCHING, BUT NOT FINDING

'Ronnie!' The name was whispered, but it penetrated the cavities of his brain with a sharpness which brought him awake in an instant.

'Mum? You OK?' Ronnie was filled with alarm.

'Sssh! Yes, I feel miles better.' Linda stood on tiptoe with her mouth to his ear. 'Come and see the dawn. It's magnificent!'

Ronnie slid to the floor without disturbing Mike, who with his back to the world was still determinedly asleep. Linda didn't seem to want him wakened either. With a finger to her lips, she drew Ronnie out into the corridor.

Ronnie remembered Ed, and wondered if he had found a rack for the night. Linda released a shutter to one of the windows, and a wispy, grey light spilled through the iron bars into the dingy corridor. 'Have you ever seen a sunrise like this?' she breathed.

'I met this bloke last night, Mum. An American called Ed. I wonder where he went,' murmured Ronnie.

'Oh, come and look,' begged Linda. She tugged him to the window.

Ronnie looked without looking, his thoughts elsewhere. Then he looked, and saw. Suddenly, India had delivered up to him yet another shock. The shock of beauty. He looked and saw a vast, still landscape spreading on and on before him; appearing and disappearing in layer after layer of milky mists. Tops of trees floated like dark islands; long-legged egrets, still as ballerinas, stood mirrored in reflecting pools; and there,, swimming into view on the farthest horizon, a thin edge of gold, wavering.

'Isn't it beautiful!' Linda sighed and leaned up against Ronnie.

This time, Ronnie didn't move away. She had wanted to share the experience with him, and him alone. He accepted it, and brief though it was, would remember it long into the future.

Mike stumbled through the doorway. 'Oh, there you are!' He sounded resentful, as someone who has been excluded.

'Oh, Mike!' Linda reacted warmly. 'Look at the sunrise. It's magical, don't you think?' She linked her arm through his.

Mike grunted. 'Yeah! Pretty impressive!' He sounded reluctant to be impressed. Ronnie walked up the corridor to see if there was any sign of Ed.

At the far end, he found the door swinging open to the outside racing by. The ticket inspector leaned, half in, half out, as if cooling himself in advance for the heat of the day which must come, as bit by bit, the giant orb lifted its flaming body into the sky.

He acknowledged Ronnie with a friendly smile and made room for him in the doorway.

'Station come soon,' said the inspector. 'Brajpur. My eldest brother lives here.'

'Oh!' Ronnie nodded, trying to show interest.

'He married,' continued the inspector, 'and has four children. All boys!' He grinned proudly. 'Now he say it high time I married.'

'You should,' agreed Ronnie.

'Oh no, no! "What kind of life?" I tell him. "I go up and down, up and down the whole of India, week after week. I would never be home. Bad for wife. Bad for children and bad for me. I'm happy. The train is my wife and my life." '

He laughed heartily at his own rhyme alliteration. 'You marry soon, huh?' He slapped Ronnie on the back with a knowing wink.

'Give us a chance!' cried Ronnie. 'I haven't even left school yet. I'm only sixteen, you know.'

'You're a man!' asserted the inspector confidently. 'My eldest brother, he ran a soap factory here in Brajpur when he was fourteen years old. He had men under him twice his age, but he was boss. He very good man.'

Ronnie made the right expressions to show he was impressed, then was glad and surprised when the inspector respected his desire for silence as he turned his attention once more to the sunrise.

The last trails of fire were free of the horizon now, and vast lakes of blue appeared amid the scarlet streaks. As rapidly as the sun rose, so people, animals and villages burst into life.

As an anonymous passenger on the train, he was like the fly on the wall, so taken for granted that he passed invisibly through their lives, free to observe without discretion. They defecated in the fields and down the embankments; they bathed themselves at pumps, in pools and at village wells; women walked with backs as straight as larches, with huge bundles on their heads, following paths that seemed to have no end; children ran with sticks chasing goats or buffalo; and the men, those who were not working the fields or opening their stalls or manning their trades, lounged on charpoys and ruminated over who knows what philosophies?

'Oh, there you are!' Mike appeared and stood between them.

Ronnie felt a stab of resentment.

'We're coming to a station soon. We'll get something to eat, and some of that awful tea, I suppose.'

The inspector laughed heartily. 'You don't like Indian tea? Eh what? We like to put everything together; tea, milk, sugar, cinnamon, cardoman – everything – and we boil it all up. Very good. You no like?'

'I no like!' said Mike firmly.

'I like it,' Ronnie said warmly.

'Ah! Very good,' and the inspector shook his head in a sideways manner which Ronnie was beginning to realise meant appreciation.

The train sidled almost inconsequentially into a small, dawn-grey rural station. A row of common brown monkeys sitting on a wall, turned their heads and stared indifferently, then resumed their task of picking lice out of each other's fur.

An old woman, bent double from years of being bent double as a sweeper, continued the only job she had ever known, brushing circular patterns into the dust with her straw brush.

A middle-aged man in a pure white dhoti, sat cross-legged on the station bench conversing with a young woman in a neatly folded, green saree. She too sat with her feet up, her chin resting on her knees, her eyes fixed intently on her companion's face. Neither glanced up as the train ground its way along the platform.

Ronnie leaned out now, hanging on to the rail, wondering if he'd catch a glimpse of Ed. Perhaps he had ridden the train without a ticket and had hidden himself from the inspector. He decided not to ask the inspector if he had seen him.

Just beyond the station platform, a young, naked boy heaved at a water pump. He jumped at each thrust, his feet swinging off the ground, so that the whole weight of his body forced out a jet of silver water under which he would then hurl himself, rubbing soap and water into his hair and face, arms and legs.

It seemed the most desirable thing in the world.

'How long have we got here?' he asked the inspector.

'Oh, thirty minutes, maybe more. We must wait here for the up train. Now you are in India, we work to IST. Indian Standard Time – or as some people say, Indian Stretchable

Time.' His laugh was infectious, and still laughing as though his sides would burst, the inspector jumped from the train. 'After all, is it not presumptuous to have a timetable at all? God has his own timetable, and whatever ones we make, in the end, it is His that we will follow. Isn't that so?' He shook his head sideways again as if in appreciation of his own logic.

'In other words,' said Ronnie. 'I have time to wash myself!'

The inspector stopped laughing and regarded him seriously. 'My dear sir, it is your duty.'

'Where are all the chai wallahs and poori wallahs?' asked Mike looking up and down the empty platform.

'This very small station, sir,' sighed the inspector. 'Just outside you find tea shacks and food.' He pointed to two low corrugated-tin-roofed mud dwellings towards which a small trickle of sleepy passengers were making their way.

Linda was looking pale again. Once she had seen the sunrise, she had returned to her bunk feeling nauseous. 'I'll stay here and guard the luggage,' she said faintly. 'Just bring me back some tea. I'd love that.'

Mike headed off towards the shacks, and Ronnie grabbed his wash bag and made for the water pump. He stripped off to his waist, then waited for the boy to finish, but the boy immediately indicated that he would work the pump for him.

Ronnie had just got himself soaped all over, when he saw Ed, jumping from the top end of the train, and running, somewhat surreptitiously, towards the shacks. 'Hey, Ed!' Ronnie waved and called.

He was sure Ed heard. He seemed to flinch momentarily, but continued running. By the time Ronnie had dashed the water from his eyes and rinsed his hair and body, there was no sign of him. He dressed quickly. 'Thanks, mate!' He smiled at the boy on the pump.

'Thanks, mate. OK,' echoed the boy cheerfully.

Ronnie ran to the other side of the station building where he had last seen Ed. There the station yard stretched out and into the street. The sun was higher and rising all the time, and with it, the temperature. Ronnie found himself panting, and stopped under a tree to take stock of his surroundings. A few bicycle rickshaw men slept, draped across their rickshaws. There would not be many customers for a while. A cow wandered about waiting for the vegetable stall to be set up. Then Ronnie saw the young man on the motor scooter. He looked so incongruous in such a rural scene, like a city slicker in his tight jeans and Empire State Building T-shirt. He sat astride his motor scooter, his legs splayed out cockily. His black hair was greased back and styled like an Indian movie star, and he viewed the world through impenetrable dark glasses so that it was impossible to know who or what he was looking at.

Then Ronnie saw Ed. He almost called out, but something made him stop and draw back slightly behind the tree. Ed wandered over casually, his hand in his jeans' pocket. When he was level with the youth on the motor scooter, he paused and they exchanged a few words. Ed drew his hand out of his pocket. It contained a packet of something. The man then drew a packet out of his jeans' pocket, and held it out. He jerked it away when Ed tried to take it, so Ed opened his packet and held it close to that the youth could see inside. At last, when it seemed that both were satisfied with the contents of each other's packets, there was a swift exchange. Then the youth turned on his engine, and with a noisy revving which startled the crows, he sped off in a cloud of dust.

Ed stood for a few moments looking after him. Then he looked around him as if to check on who might have seen him. He didn't notice Ronnie, who had stepped back out of sight behind the tree.

Ed walked, faster this time as if to some purpose, back to the station buildings.

Ronnie felt awkward. He hadn't intended to spy, yet he was spying. He didn't want to follow Ed, yet he wanted to make contact with him again. He was both curious and attracted to him. There was a lot he could ask him about India.

He lost sight of him for a few moments, and hurried on to the station platform. The man in the white dhoti and the woman in the green saree were still there talking intently. As he passed by they stared at him, long and hard, and Ronnie felt resentment at their rudeness. Then the woman said something. He heard the word "Britisher" and they laughed. Like Ed, they recognised him for what he was – perhaps also for what he was not – neither English nor Indian. He scowled angrily.

There was a narrow alley running down the side of the station. Ronnie wasn't sure what made him go over. Perhaps a shadow, a flash of blond hair. Feeling he might be intruding, he peered round the corner. It smelt powerfully of drains. Ronnie retched and drew back, but not before he glimpsed him, Ed, crouched in a doorway; not before he had seen the syringe poised above a vein in his left lower arm squeezed between the thumb and forefinger.

Ronnie was glad when the train got under way again. He moved down to the far end of the corridor and stared sullenly at the parched countryside with slow-moving figures. The sun was climbing steadily.

'Hey! There you are! I looked out for you!' Once again Ed had materialised, it seemed from nowhere. Ronnie studied him closely with suspicion. Ed's whole frame filled the corridor. His eyes glittered with a feverish brightness, and his muscles seemed to be flexed with an almost excess energy. He rocked to and fro on his heels. He looked tall and golden. Not the sub-human creature who had crouched near the drains.

Ronnie looked at the inside of his arms. He saw the bruised, swollen veins and the red smudges where countless needles had gone in. He thought, 'That's a lie.'

'Get some tea?' asked Ed.

111

'No. Didn't want any. Enjoy your fix?' Ronnie hadn't meant to say it, but the words fell bitterly from his lips.

'What's it to you?' Ed's eyes narrowed.

Ronnie shook his head dumbly.'Sorry,' he muttered. 'It's nothing to me.' Then he said, 'You didn't look the sort, that's all.'

'Oh. You know the sort, do you?' Ed sounded taunting. 'Tell me what they're like.'

'Self-centred,' commented Ronnie. 'Suicidal. You suicidal? You seemed interested in totting up points to get you to Nirvana – or whatever it is. Do you rob and steal? Where do you get the money?'

'Hey, hey! What's biting you?' Ed sounded almost gentle. 'Let me tell you, kid. I don't want to die. I simply got hooked. It seemed the only thing left for me to try. You see, I'm one of life's experimenters. I want to know. I want to experience. Everything.'

'Oh,' Ronnie said flatly. 'I just thought you had more sense.' He turned his back on him.

'You've known someone on drugs, haven't you?' Ed spoke softly.

Ronnie shrugged. 'He's dead.'

'Well, that's why I'm out here. I want to stay alive – but – I need a reason. Something more than just making money. That's all they think about back home. Making it big. Well, I did all that. I made it big. You thought I had more sense? I may not have sense, but I had brains. I was top in my year at Harvard. Graduated with my MBA and made my first sixty thousand bucks by the time I was twenty-three. I was a great yuppy. My dad's promised me his company by the time I'm thirty. I married a top society girl. I'm a father, you know. Got a kid.' He kicked the side of the corridor. 'Yeah! I got all right. I got, I got. But what have I got? You tell me? What do I do with the rest of my life? You ask them out there.' He pointed to India. 'You ask them what I'm doing in India, and they'll tell you.' He whirled round to the carriage behind them. The man and woman who had been sitting on the bench at the last station occupied it and were still carrying on their conversation. They glanced up, but only to show contempt and returned their attention to each other. 'You ask them what I'm doing in India and they'll tell you. They'll say I'm another of the thousands of Western hippies who've begged, borrowed and stolen their way across India. Been robbed of all their money by false gurus. Another rich American who thought he could buy his way to Nirvana, but who took drugs instead and landed up, that most despicable of all creatures, a white man begging on the streets of Calcutta.

'I could live another five decades – but for what? There has to be more to life than making money and raising kids to help them make money. I don't believe in God – damn it, but I've got to believe there's something more than Mammon. Can you get to heaven if you're a yuppy?'

Ronnie still had his back to him. Ed touched his shoulder. 'Do you still despise me?'

'No. Perhaps my dad felt the same. Perhaps that's why he left us. My mum and me. I never really understood it before.Perhaps . . .' his voice trailed away.

'Yeah! Perhaps,' Ed nodded eagerly. 'Perhaps he did.'

'Where are you going?' asked Ronnie. Turning to face him, it was a begin-at-the-beginning question really.

'Oh!' The American shook his head vaguely. 'I don't know any more. I'm not really going anywhere now. I'm searching, but not finding, so I'm probably on my way home, in a slow roundabout way. Like all the rest, I came hoping to find a guru who could give me the answer. I was given names. I visited ashrams. I listened, I learned, I tried. But none of it was any good to me. I'm still searching.'

'I wonder if I'll be in that predicament in a few weeks' or months' time; looking, searching and not finding.'

'But at least you know what you're looking for. It's your dad, isn't it?'

'Yeah. We think he's in India. I want to find him.'

'Sure. Of course you do, and he's tangible, and no doubt you've got a lead. Something to go on. At least you know what station you're getting off at, and why. Me – my leads have run out. I'm counting on luck now. I've thrown myself on to the roulette wheel and hope I come up with the lucky number. You get off at the next stop, don't you? Durgapur?'

'It's where my father was found and adopted,' said Ronnie. 'We hope we'll find people still alive who'll remember. Perhaps one of the missionaries – there's one still alive in an old people's home there. Then there's Charlie, the dog catcher. He's the one who knew about the singing bowls. Perhaps there's someone who knew him who can help.'

'Singing bowls?' Ed murmured. Intrigued. 'What about them?'

Ronnie felt reticent. He regretted having mentioned them. 'They were just some old bowls which came with my father as a baby. We thought they might be a clue.' He tried to sound offhand and casual.

The pupils in Ed's eyes were so dilated now the blue looked black. He stared at Ronnie, though Ronnie wasn't sure if it was him that he saw.

'Do they sing? Do they sing like birds?' Ed began waving his arms and backing down the corridor.

Ronnie watched with growing alarm. He'd never been close to anyone under the influence of drugs.

Ed reached the door and suddenly threw it open. India rushed by with the clattering of wheels and the shriek of the train's whistle. Ed grabbed the rail with one hand and swung his whole body outwards. 'Yahoo!' he whooped like a cowboy.

'I could fly, Ronnie! I could fly! Do you want to see me?'

'Ed! Don't!' Ronnie rushed forward. He grabbed the hand which held the rail. 'Don't be stupid. For God's sake, come in!'

Ed swung about, whooping and yahooing. 'I can sing, too! "Oh, give me a home, where the buffaloes roam, where the deer and the antelope play . . ." ' he shouted his song into the outside. ' "Where seldom is heard a discouraging word, and the skies are not cloudy all day!" ' He pulled himself in and stood with his back to the open doorway. He leaned forward till his face nearly touched Ronnie's. 'Bet your bowls don't sing as good as me.'

Ronnie tugged him inwards and kicked the door shut behind him. 'You're mad!' he said bitterly. 'You need to see a bloody psychiatrist. Get dried out. Anyhow, I'm not staying around to watch you kill yourself. If I were you, Ed, I'd go home!'

Ronnie pressed his arm with a sudden rush of compassion, then left him. He walked down the corridor to his own compartment, and didn't look back.

16
DÉJÀ VU

Durgapur. The name on the station platform swam, slow motion, into view. Immediately, Ronnie felt the shock of recognition.

The moment his feet touched the platform; the moment he smelt the whiff of Indian tobacco; saw the monkeys leaping over the station roof; the ubiquitous black crow, ever present, ever watchful, Ronnie was overwhelmed by a feeling of *déjà vu.* 'I have been here before, but where or how I cannot tell, I know the grass before the door, the sweet keen smell . . .' the lines of a poem learned at school came vividly back to him.

He felt Henry's presence everywhere. Henry would have known every bit of this station. Five years he had been stationed here, travelling to and from Durgapur to Lucknow or Delhi, to Calcutta or Lahore. And after he had been rescued by the forest hermit and his daughter – 'my great-grandfather and my grandmother,' Ronnie reminded himself – Henry had followed a railway track out of the forest back to Durgapur. Probably this very railway track. Ronnie's eyes followed the shimmering rails out of the shade of the covered station, into the glare of the noon sun where they ran, too bright to follow any more into a dazzling haze of distance. Ronnie felt the urge to follow. They were right to come. Now he knew it. Now he felt it and wondered how he had ever doubted.

Suddenly, Henry's presence was overwhelming. 'Take the bowls and find him,' he could hear his voice urging him; the last words he would ever hear him say.

'Have we got everything?' asked Ronnie. He had been checking their belongings as they came off the train.

'Yeah! But what do we do now!' sighed Mike bleakly. He glanced anxiously at Linda. 'We've got to get your mother to a bed and to a doctor.'

'I was hoping someone would meet us,' said Linda plaintively. I wrote to the hospital. I know that still exists. The missionaries have all gone long ago. I had a vague reply from a Dr Prasad who said he would make enquiries . . . but,' her voice trailed off pessimistically.

The train inspector hovered round them sympathetically. 'You take rickshaw and go to Claridges Hotel. First-class hotel. Very good. Very clean. It's run by my cousin, Mr Dalal. You stay there and look after the Mrs. She not good. My cousin will find you first-class doctor, yes?'

'Thanks,' grunted Mike, taking the hand that was offered him. 'Yeah, thanks.' For once, Ronnie felt that he meant it. 'I reckon that guy's got relatives at every station up and down the railway system of India. Probably all a rip-off. Still, we've got to go somewhere.' And Mike heaved his rucksack on to his back, and then took Linda's over his shoulder.

Ronnie scanned the length of the train wondering if he would catch a glimpse of Ed. Perhaps he's hurled himself off the train. Was lying dead somewhere back along the track. Ronnie bit his lip. No. Not Ed. It didn't really fit. There was no sign of him among the clusters of families and passengers surging on and off the train. He was probably sleeping it off somewhere. Ronnie put him out of his mind.

Slowly they moved off the platform, through the cool ticket hall and out into the blazing glare and heat of the station forecourt.

For a town the size of Durgapur they might have expected a taxi rank, or some form of motorised vehicles, but instead, apart from an ancient Ambassador car slumped in a corner, the main form of public transport seemed to be the bicycle rickshaw.

'What would Grandpa have done?' wondered Ronnie. 'Probably be met by some official car and swept away in style.'

The three of them surveyed the conglomeration of brightly coloured rickshaws. The drivers had straightened themselves out from their sleeping positions, had rewound their turbans, adjusted their dhotis, and sat astride their bicycles each vying competitively with the other for custom. They watched how the other passengers wandered over, selected a rickshaw of their choice, entered into a swift bargain then climbed on board. Two, sometimes three people, luggage and all, climbed on to one rickshaw. Ronnie was both amazed and appalled to see the thin, scrawny bodies of the cyclists heave into action, with every muscle and sinew in their bodies tightening like knots of rope with the effort.

'We're taking one each,' said Linda firmly. 'Those poor men! It shouldn't be allowed.'

Mike walked over to them trying to look authoritative. He approached a man who looked a bit older than the rest. There were flecks of grey in his hair, and some of his teeth were missing. Instinctively, Mike thought perhaps he would be less likely to be dishonest than the younger men.

'Claridges Hotel. How much?' he demanded.

'Thirty rupees,' replied the man getting down off his bicycle and preparing to pile on the rucksacks.

'You come with me, sir!' cried another. 'I take you for twenty-five rupees. I go faster. He too old.'

The old man was not to be outdone. After a swift consultation with another driver, he said, 'Forty-five rupees for two. You need two, yes?' he added looking at all three of them with their rucksacks, and again, he attempted to start piling them on.

'Hold it, hold it!' cried Mike, realising he was losing control of the situation. What had the guide book said about bargaining? Assume that they have started at double the real rate, offer less than half, then take it up to an agreed compromise.

'Twenty rupees for two,' stated Mike.

'No, no!' said the elderly rickshaw man, appearing to give up. 'No good.' The others nodded in agreement. Mike began to walk away, but he felt he had no cards to play. Who else could he go to? Then to his relief another voice called out.

'Thirty-five for the two, sir. I take you all, him and me,' he pointed to another man, even older than the first Mike had approached.

'This is ridiculous,' muttered Mike. 'The man is probably less than half my weight.'

He was about to turn back and accept the younger man, even if it meant paying more, when a roar as loud as an aeroplane shattered the hot stillness of the afternoon. They looked in astonishment as a huge, bulky, black motorbike, an old Norton, came hurtling into the forecourt, raced round the perimeter and skidded to a stop with a spray of dust before them at the bottom of the steps.

A crouched figure in helmet, goggles and leather flying jacket, looking for all the world like Biggles, leapt off the machine and bounded up the steps towards them.

'You are Henry Saville Sahib's family?' he cried, pulling back his goggles and undoing the helmet.

They found themselves staring into the cheerful, chubby, perspiring face of an Indian somewhere in his middle years.

'Yes!' cried Ronnie eagerly.

'I'm his daughter-in-law, this is Ronnie, his grandson,' added Linda. 'This is a good friend,' she indicated Mike.

Mike nodded curtly. 'Have you come to meet us, then?'

'Dr Prasad told me you were coming. I have made arrangements. My name is Prem Singh. My father was Ram Singh, Mr

Saville Sahib's bearer. You come with me, now. I take you to his bungalow.'

He swaggered over to the rickshaw wallahs, selected two of them and agreed a price with a mere nod of the head.

'How much are they taking us for?' asked Mike curiously.

'Four rupees each,' said Prem Singh,' and not one rupee more. OK?'

'Four rupees,' cried Mike weakly, 'and I was about to pay thirty-five.'

'Ronnie! You like to ride on the Norton with me? This was Henry Saville Sahib's motorbike. He leave it for my father and now I ride it.'

The feeling of *déjà vu* strengthened as he climbed on to the pillion behind Prem Singh. There was a peculiar familiarity to the tarmaced roads, the roundabouts and intersections and traffic islands; the low-lying bungalows with their pitched, tiled roofs and deep verandahs, maintaining their English sense of privacy behind hedges and shrubs and flowering jacaranda and flame of the forest. Any moment now, he thought that a memsahib would appear in her broad-rimmed hat and secateurs to prune the roses and give orders to the gardener. And there was the church, red brick and white-timbered, with a spire reaching confidently Heavenwards proclaiming the superiority of the Established Church. Yes, this had been Henry Saville's India. But so was the bazaar. They crossed over Napier Road – and British India was left behind for the moment.

Prem Singh enjoyed the effect he created as he roared into the bazaar. Ronnie heard him whooping with relish as children, chickens, street vendors, dogs, cows and all manner of livestock scattered before his path.

Being the only machine on the road, he had priority over such vehicles which were man-drawn, horse-drawn, cycle-drawn or bullock-drawn. They knew it and he knew it. No bureaucrat in Delhi compiling a Western-style highway code counted out here. Here there was a well-defined, and well-understood pecking order which decreed that the fastest and most powerful vehicle always had priority.

Ronnie laughed out loud with amusement and exhilaration as they tore recklessly into the crowded streets. Prem Singh swore and cursed and hooted his horn.

Laughter turned to a warning shout. Ronnie saw him. He shut his eyes in horror. They couldn't possibly avoid him. A long, thin, scarecrow-like figure just stepped out in front of them. A blur of saffron robe.

There was a burning smell of brakes; Prem Singh hurled the machine sideways. Ronnie heard horrified cries. He felt himself slide from the machine and for a second, become airborne. He felt no pain. No physical sensation at all, not until hands fluttered over him, touching, stroking, calming, lifting.

Prem Singh came thrusting through the jostling onlookers. 'Oh my goodness, Mr Ronnie! Are you OK? That fool of a sadhu. He walks out as if he thinks he's immortal. Any bones broken? Can you walk? Oh my goodness.'

They were outside a grain shop. The merchant and his wife brought a chair out on to the wooden verandah, and Ronnie was ushered to it by a flurry of helpful hands. A glass of water was offered him, and he drank, then realised he shouldn't have as it wouldn't be sterilised. 'I'm fine! I'm fine!' he insisted.

Everyone was discussing the incident, Prem Singh gesticulating and re-enacting the whole event. Ronnie could hear his voice protesting and accusing, and the words "bloody" and "stupid fool" permeating his diatribe.

As if at a signal, the hubbub died abruptly away. The crowd fell back and a path opened up among them. Sitting up on the rickety platform, Ronnie felt suddenly exposed, as walking through the crowd, in a deliberate line coming straight towards him, was the thin, scarecrow-like, blur of saffron robe – a holy man.

Ronnie half rose apologetically. 'I'm sorry . . .' he murmured.

The holy man either didn't hear him, or ignored his apology. He raised his stick, and Ronnie braced himself instinctively for a blow. But no blow came. The holy man lightly touched him on the forehead with the end of his stick and held him in an hypnotic gaze. He spoke some words in Urdu, nodded and looked at him piercingly. Then he turned and walked away through the crowd which closed behind him and swallowed him from view.

'What did he say?' asked Ronnie, bewildered.'What did he say? Tell me!' Prem Singh came up, relaxed and smiling cheerfully once more. He looked vindicated, and he confidently brushed down his lapels, adjusted his helmet and gestured to Ronnie to get on to the motorbike. 'He speak some silly nonsense. Most of these fellows are cracked, you know. You mustn't take notice too much.'

'But tell me what he said. I want to know,' urged Ronnie.

'Oh, it was nothing. Just something about you searching. Yes – he say, you are searching and you will find. That's all!' he grinned. 'We are all searching, aren't we?'

'That's all!' Ronnie murmured. 'Yes . . . I suppose we are!' He scanned the crowded bazaar looking for some sign of the holy man, but he had disappeared.

'Come, sir Ronnie. Your mother and Mr Mike will get there before us and that would never do. Those rickshaw wallahs would laugh their heads off to think they had beaten my Norton motorbike!'

Ronnie smiled his thanks to the merchant and his wife, and they nodded and rolled their shoulders amicably in return.

Prem Singh revved up loudly to re-establish his status on the road.

Everyone drew back to give him plenty of room. Ronnie climbed up on the pillion once more, and with a loud tooting, they sped away.

'You are searching. You will find.' Did the holy man really say that? He remembered Ed. He shivered. Not with dread or foreboding. Just a feeling that somehow, bit by bit, ever since he had found the singing bowls, he was being pulled along by another hand. Everything was pre-ordained.

The motorbike and the holy man, they were no accident, and when the large metal-spiked gate of the District Commissioner's bungalow loomed into sight, it was not as a stranger that Ronnie entered the compound.

It was as if he had been here before. He knew the gate would squeal when it swung slowly open; he knew the simple shelter where the night watchman used to sit smoking his hookah through the night. He knew the long, winding drive down to the bungalow, situated at the farthest and broadest end of the compound, where all the villagers could gather each fortnight to receive their wheat and rice rations, and he knew the low-roofed dwellings of the servants' quarters, and the great broad-shaded tamarind tree.

He knew the bungalow. There was still much dignity left to this old English Colonial building, though the white plaster work was faded and pitted, and the windows stared out blankly like sad eyes.

The verandah, too, had a desolate look to it, as if grieving for those hospitable days when the evening air rang with English voices, the clunk of cocktail glasses and talk of 'back home'. The once immaculate lawns were brown and threadbare, the flower-beds long since dried up and barren; yet the compound had been jealously guarded from squatters, vagrants, wandering cows, and the political daubings and grafitti of student activities.

Prem Singh drew up in front of the verandah steps. Ronnie got off and stood at the bottom step where the shrubbery was thick and profuse. He knew this, too.

'I'll open up,' exclaimed Prem Singh, pulling out a large key from his pocket. We must let in some light and air before the Mrs and Mr Mike come, yes?'

He pulled open an outer wire-meshed door, and then with the key, opened the inner wooden door. He fixed both at an opened position with wooden wedges. Ronnie came and stood in the threshold. A shaft of light cut a swathe through the gloom and revealed the cool, high-ceilinged rooms from which hung old, dusty fans, silent and immobile as if trapped by the cobwebs which festooned the blades. He could feel Henry's presence everywhere, and although the bungalow was stripped bare, Ronnie, wandering from room to room, soon furnished it in his imagination, and brought young Henry Saville in to inhabit it once more.

'Mr Saville Sahib?' an old voice called tremulously through the gloom. Ronnie, see-sawing backwards and forwards in time, hardly knew whether it was his grandfather who was being summoned or himself. He waited, dazed.

'Mr Saville Sahib?' The voice called again, a little nearer. Ronnie heard a shuffling on the verandah. He walked back to the open door. An old man stood at the top of the verandah steps, his hair clinging like snow to his brown, wrinkled brow and his dark, glittering eyes darting eagerly, searching for the visitor.

Ronnie appeared in the doorway.

'Mr Saville Sahib?' The old man spoke the name again and again, as if it had lain reluctantly dormant on his tongue all these years.

'I'm Ronnie Saville,' said Ronnie. 'Henry Saville's grandson.'

With a rush of affection, the old man reached forward and clasped both Ronnie's hands in his. 'I am very happy to meet Mr Saville Sahib's grandson Ronnie!' He spoke the word "Ronnie" with a warmth and richness. It gave the nickname a distinction which Ronnie had never been aware of before.

'Oh why, oh why did you not bring your grandfather back with you? He was my friend. Why did he not return to visit his old servant before he died?'

'Ram Singh? Are you Ram Singh?' exclaimed Ronnie.

'Yes, yes! Your grandfather was a very good man. You are the proof!' He looked up at the tall, young boy who towered above him and his eyes filled with tears. 'Come, come!' He gripped Ronnie's arm urgently. 'See over there!' He pointed beyond the tamarind tree towards the low outer wall of the compound. 'That is where I first saw your father! Oh, Ram, Ram! What a day that was. Hidden he was, in the saree of an old woman covered with smallpox. How could he survive?' Ram Singh fell silent as he remembered.

'Tell me more,' whispered Ronnie.

The old man nodded his head slowly as if there were too many memories to carry around. 'He must have been blessed by the gods – this child of the forest.'

'Father!' Prem Singh appeared looking pleased with himself. 'I have prepared the old guest rooms for our visitors, but they must have clean water. Did Mother boil a saucepan as I asked?'

'Yes, yes!' the old man answered. 'My son Prem Singh!' He introduced him proudly.

'We've met, Papa!' Prem Singh reminded him patiently. 'I've just brought him from the station on the Norton! His mother and a friend, Mr Mike, are following in rickshaws.'

'Tell me more,' begged Ronnie.

'Yes! Come!' The old man took Ronnie's arm and led him down the verandah steps. 'Let me take you to the very spot, and I will tell you more.' The young boy and the old man walked slowly across the compound while Prem hurried towards the old servants' quarters to organise food and water.

Prem Singh had produced a table, chairs, a white cloth and a full set of crockery and cutlery, and by the time Mike and Linda came trundling down the drive in their rickshaws, a delicious smell of rice and curry drifted across the compound.

Mike leapt out exhiliarated. 'Some of these fellows should be entered for the Olympics!' he declared. 'Their muscle power is amazing!' He pulled out a wodge of notes from his pocket and gave each man ten rupees.

'Darling, isn't that too much?' cried Linda. She hadn't moved from her seat, trying desperately to fight off the nausea that was sweeping over her.

125

'Missus right,' agreed Prem Singh. 'These men get greedy if you pay too much. Upset local economy.'

'Well, I think they deserve it,' insisted Mike patronisingly. He was beginning to enjoy himself.

Linda climbed slowly out of the rickshaw, while Prem Singh heaved off their rucksacks.

'Thanks, chaps!' exclaimed Mike as the men wheeled their bikes round towards the exit.

The men salaamed almost curtly, then cycled swiftly away as if afraid Mike might change his mind.

'Well, I must say, the British certainly knew how to live when they were in India,' breathed Mike admiringly as he studied the bungalow. 'No wonder they didn't want to leave. I wouldn't mind leading this sort of life myself.' And he ran up the verandah steps and flung himself down in a cane chair which Prem Singh had brought out. 'Yes! I think I could get quite a taste for it.' He tossed his legs up on to the table.

'Oh, stop it, Mike,' frowned Linda. 'Don't start behaving like an Imperialist.' She stared beyond the tamarind tree where Ronnie and the old man walked on the periphery of the compound. From a distance Ronnie looked like his father. He even walked the same way, his shoulders nervously stiff and his hands gesticulating in front as if their gestures added to his vocabulary. An old feeling stirred inside her. She and Adam had met at university. He had been only three years older than Ronnie now, and had looked much the same – tall and angular, and anxious to be courteous. If only . . . She shook herself impatiently at her own regrets . . . If only nothing. Life could be full of 'if onlys'. He was what he was, and nothing – not she, not even Henry and Isabella could change what he was inside. Yet, if only she had been, perhaps more mature, more aware, she might have been able to keep pace with the searching that had gone on inside him. Perhaps she hadn't loved him enough. And now? What would she feel now if he were suddenly to walk across the compound? She could remember what it had been like to love him.

'Darling, you look pale,' Mike was by her side. He put his arm round her firmly. 'Do you think you can manage something to eat, or should you lie down? I'll get a doctor to you tomorrow, unless,' he looked at her closely, 'unless you feel I should find one right away?'

'No, no!' She wriggled from his hold. 'I'm all right for the moment. I won't eat though, that would be stupid. I'd just like to sit a while in the shade. I'm quite happy.'

Mike felt her rejection and scowled. He was a fool to come. A fool to let her come. It was bound to stir up all sorts of things; memories. He flung himself back in the cane chair. 'As you like,' he said sulkily.

Then suddenly Prem Singh was back accompanied by three little children all carrying pails of water. 'Now you can bathe,' he said cheerily. Ram Singh and Ronnie also returned, their faces quietly happy with exchanged information.

'Mum! This is Ram Singh! Grandpa's old servant. He was there when they found Dad!'

Ram Singh came forward reverentially and knelt at her feet. 'Dear lady!' he murmured. 'I am most honoured to meet you. Mr Henry Saville Sahib was more than a good master to me. He was my friend. I never had a chance to show my gratitude – till now. Anything you want – any of you – you just speak, and I or Prem Singh or his wife, Muni, all of us will be at your service.'

Embarrassed, but moved by his declaration, Linda took his hands and urged him to rise. 'I am very glad to meet you, too. I just wish that . . .' her voice trailed away. It would have been so much better if Henry had come or . . .

'Did . . .' she hardly dared ask. 'Did he – Adam – Ronnie's father . . .' she indicated her son. 'Did he come here? Looking?'

Ram Singh looked anguished. 'Alas, madam, I know not. I had no means of knowing what he looked like. No man came to me. No man who looked like Ronnie. Then perhaps he had

127

already put on Indian dress – or even the garments of a *sanyasi* – a disciple. I would not know him.'

'I see.'

'Madam,' Prem Singh interrupted her thoughts. 'Will you eat? Or would you rather rest. I show you room, yes?'

'I will rest now,' she said quietly, and allowed him to lead her to a room at the far end of the verandah.

The three young children appeared again, this time bearing trays of food. Coils of delicious steam rose from the dish of fluffy boiled rice, while more pungent and mouth-watering smells invaded their nostrils from the others.

Prem Singh had set a table inside. He shut the wire-mesh door to keep out the mosquitoes and other insects, and left the children sitting on the verandah outside, ready to fetch and carry.

Mike and Ronnie tried to talk over the meal. They admired the cooking. They expressed their delight at having come to such a hospitable place. But each had his own thoughts. They could not communicate with each other and they soon lapsed into silence.

When they had finished, the children came in bobbing and grinning and whispering to each other and giggling, and soon took everything away. Then Mike went along to see how Linda was and Ronnie walked out on to the verandah.

Déjà vu. The Indian night spread before him like an aural tapestry of sound. He heard what Henry would have heard. The crickets – a million-strong chorus, throbbed like the night's pulse beat. From the direction of the servants' quarters came a gentle singing and the tired voices of little children, and up the drive, beyond the gate, the delicate clip-clop of Indian horses and the insistent tring-tring of the bicycle bells. A distant drum beat added its own rhythm to the night accompanied by the occasional tinkle of bells.

'Ronnie!'

128

Ronnie was startled. *Déjà vu.* He turned but saw no one. Then old Ram Singh shuffled up the steps into the light of the bobbing kerosene lantern.

'Ronnie, you have the singing bowls? They came with your father, yes?' The old man looked at him with his head on one side, eyebrows raised in anticipation.

'Yes, yes. I do have them. Shall I get them out?'

It was right to get them out. Here of all places and on a night like this. Ram Singh looked excited. His eyes glittered and he rubbed his hands.

'Wait here,' said Ronnie, and he went into the bungalow to find his rucksack. 'Only two?' asked Ram Singh, as Ronnie carried them out and placed them on the table.

'We think my father took one when he left.'

'Ah!' The old man nodded and fell silent, but his eyes never left Ronnie as he sat down in front of the bowls.

'Sit down!' Ronnie indicated the other chair.

With a rapid movement of delight, the old man sat down and drew himself in as close to the bowls as he could.

'Play!' he whispered.

Suddenly Ronnie felt afraid. 'The last time I played the bowls was the night my grandfather died.'

'Play, play!' Ram Singh urged.

Ronnie stretched out his fingers and let the tips rest lightly on the rim of the smaller bowl. The alloy of ancient metals – gold, silver, brass and copper merged with the metal contained within his own body. Slowly, slowly, his fingers began to rotate around the rim. At first there was no audible sound, then like the distant beginnings of time itself, a round shape of a sound formed beneath his touch and expanded.

'Ôm!' breathed Ram Singh. He had closed his eyes and was rocking slightly as the sound increased.

Now Ronnie put more pressure on the rim. He felt the bowl quiver and a vibrato of sound ran up his arm and spread like an electric current through his body. Round and round and round and round. His fingers were rotating: the whole world was rotating; spinning with the sound. On and on. There was no reason to stop. On and on. It was a summoning call. Who knows who or what he could bring before him. On and on. He felt a stab of pain, or was it fear? 'Grandpa.' He snatched his fingers from the rim. The sound hung on the air with a life of its own. What if it refused to die? Ronnie blocked his ears. He sensed a movement and saw Ram Singh looking at him with tear-filled eyes. He took his hands away and heard the last pulsating note dying away until there was silence. The Indian night throbbed on; but there was silence.

'Thank you.' Ram Singh got to his feet holding the table for support. The tears rolled down his cheeks. Slowly he moved to the edge of the verandah and, one tread at a time, made his way down the steps.

Ronnie stayed seated. He cupped both hands round the bowl and drew it to his chest. The sound had gone, and yet it lived on and on, re-echoing in the recesses of his mind.

'Ronnie!' His name again? He could see Ram Singh's bent figure dwindling into the night.

'Who's there?' He strained to see beyond the circle of the lamplight.

The darkness seemed to spread for ever and ever. 'Grandpa?'

Then a shape separated itself from the greater shape of the tamarind tree. It moved forward, visible and invisible.

As if for protection, Ronnie took up the kerosene lamp and held it out before him. The feeble light gave substance to the shape. Tall, upright, almost golden in the wavering glow.

'Ed!'

17
PAUSE BEFORE ACTION

Instinctively, Ronnie lowered the lantern and stepped back to block the bowls from view. Yet he knew it was useless. He and Ed stood appraising each other across the gulf of darkness between them.

Ronnie thought the silence would last for ever, then Ed drawled softly, 'You don't mind if I bed down here for the night, do you? I've had it with bloody trains and station platforms.'

Ronnie hesitated with suspicion, then he shrugged, the briefest of shrugs. Ed smiled and strolled forwards with the studied nonchalance of a predator. His long legs leapt the verandah steps in one, and without even glancing at the bowls on the table, he selected himself a spot on the corner just before the verandah curved round to the back of the bungalow. Here, he tossed down his rucksack and began extricating his sleeping bag and cotton sheet.

Ronnie watched impassively, as the American rooted round and round like a dog in its basket, till he had moulded himself into a comfortable position. Then, abruptly, without a last look or word, he became inanimate.

A held breath. The night, too, was inanimate. The pause before action.

Suddenly, the breath was expelled once more, the breathing resumed, and what had seemed like silence was after all nothing but a temporary paralysis of the aural senses. The notes of the singing bowls rippled on into the night, and nocturnal sounds came in waves once more, lapping and over-lapping.

Ronnie collected up the bowls and took them to his room.

Prem Singh had rigged up a mosquito net for him over a broad, old bed with an oak headboard. Henry's bed. Ronnie crawled inside, taking the bowls with him and placed them near his pillow, within reach.

'Dad!' Ronnie knew he had shouted out. He waited for someone to respond, but no one did. He would have said he hadn't slept, were it not for the grey light which now edged the shuttered windows, and the wild chorus of dawn birds shaking the tamarind tree.

He remembered Ed and with a sudden panic rolled over to touch the bowls. They were still there.

He heard the kick of the motorbike and a murmur of voices. Ronnie threw back the mosquito net and ran out to investigate.

He met Mike coming across the compound from the servants' quarters. He looked dishevelled and unrested, his face creased with apprehension. 'I've just sent Prem Singh for the doctor. Linda's had a rotten night.' He pushed his hand wearily through his hair. Their eyes met briefly, and Ronnie expected to be blamed once more, but instead his expression was of one almost pleading for reassurance. 'God, I hope she'll be all right. I hope the doctor will know what to do.'

'Can I see her?' asked Ronnie gently.

'Yup, but just go quietly, in case she's dropped off. She's absolutely exhausted.'

Ronnie went to her room. 'Mum?' He sat anxiously on the bed. Her face gleamed white against the white sheets, and there was a smell of vomit and perspiration.

She reached out for his hand. 'I'm sorry, love.' Her eyes brimmed with despair.

'It's not your fault. I'm the one who should be sorry. I shouldn't have made you come. Mike was right.' Ronnie's shoulders slumped with uncertainty.

'No, love. You had to come. We had to come,' Linda struggled to sit up. 'Maybe I shouldn't have persuaded Mike. He hates it. I just felt I couldn't manage unless he came along; but we both need to know, don't we?' She shook his arm. 'Don't we?'

Ronnie looked at her searchingly. She nodded. 'We have to know, Ronnie, if there's a chance of knowing.'

'Yeah!' He squeezed her hand in return. 'Just get better, Mum, so we can carry on looking.'

'Ronnie!' Mike stood in the doorway, puffed with indignation. 'Some bloody hippy's parked himself on our verandah. Do you know him?'

'Sort of,' Ronnie answered guardedly. 'His name's Ed McGill. He's an American I met on the train. He came last night and asked to kip on the verandah. I didn't see why not. He's not doing any harm, is he?'

Mike shook his head with the superiority of the experienced over the idiot. 'Get rid of him, that's all,' he snapped.

'Bloody hell!' Ronnie leapt to his feet, shaking away Linda's restraining hand. 'Who the hell do you think you are?'

'Ronnie!' Linda's voice rose in anguish. 'Don't quarrel, please!' She turned to Mike. 'Please, Mike!'

'No, Linda! We don't want any hippies hanging round our necks. It's bad enough with you being ill. Blokes like that make me puke. Spongers, that's all they are. Nothing but trouble wherever they go!'

'Hey, come on!' Ronnie protested. 'You haven't even met the guy. You don't know anything about him.'

'I don't care if he's the bloody Mahatma Gandhi, I want him out.' Mike paced across the room. 'Will you do it, or shall I?'

'Mike!' Linda swung her legs out of bed. She made to get up.

'What the hell are you doing?' Mike rushed over to restrain her. 'Come on, love. Back to bed.' His voice became suddenly tender as he eased her among the pillows.

'We'll sort it out. I'm sorry I got mad.' He patted her gently.

Ronnie strode out of the room, his fists clenched by his side. He was shocked at how violent Mike could make him feel. He leaned on the verandah wall in despair. How were they ever going to continue the search?

Mike appeared, his body still stiff with anger. Ronnie turned to face him.

'Breakfast!' They were interrupted by Prem Singh's young children, their voices chiming across the compound as they came trotting along bearing silver platters with lids, and trays with plates and cutlery and condiments. Muni brought up the rear carrying a spotlessly white tablecloth draped across her arms.

She glided up the verandah steps shining with smiles and swept between Mike and Ronnie.

They continued to glare at each other like combatants interrupted mid-fight. Beyond them, inside, Muni tossed the white tablecloth over the grimy table while the children lifted the lids from the platters and released a multitude of smells from the omelettes and sausages, parathas and curried potatoes.

There was a commotion up at the gate. A nasal horn beeped impatiently and an engine revved with excessive exuberance. A child opened the gate just wide enough to let Prem Singh through on his motorbike, and the birds in the tamarind tree flew outwards with a great shriek as he roared down the drive.

'Well! Did you find a doctor?' Mike asked eagerly.

134

'Doctor coming,' Prem Singh beamed, pushing back his goggles.

'Is he English?'

'No, no. All English doctors gone long time ago. Dr Bailey, he stayed on, but he dead now, three years ago.'

'Oh!' Ronnie groaned with disappointment. Three years ago. Why didn't they know Dr Bailey was dead, this man who had nursed his father as a baby? Ronnie felt cheated.

'Don't worry!' Prem Singh was concerned to reassure them. 'Dr Prasad very good doctor. Very brainworthy doctor. Dr Bailey sponsored him to study in England. He's arriving soon in a tonga.'

Then Prem Singh noticed Ed still curled up asleep on the verandah. 'Friend?' he asked curiously.

'No,' said Mike curtly.

'Yes,' replied Ronnie simultaneously. 'I met him on the train. He's an American.'

'Hmmm!' Prem Singh shook his head doubtfully. 'Watch out for hippies,' he advised. 'Always looking for drugs; always stealing and begging for money to get drugs. We in India, we very amazed at this, when we see Westerners coming to India. We had no idea white people could beg and become so low. We very amazed and disappointed. Very bad. Very bad.' He sucked in his cheeks disapprovingly.

'Yeah!' Mike was triumphant. 'That's what I've been saying. I agree with you, Prem Singh. They're nothing but trouble, but try telling this boy!'

A tonga halted at the closed gate. Prem Singh shouted and a child ran out from nowhere to open it, cadging a ride on the bars as it swung back.

Dr Prasad had arrived. The small, bony, plumed horse tritt-trotted down the drive. Even before its old hunched driver had brought it to a halt, a slight, very dark, sharp-featured man leapt from the carriage. He clutched an ancient, battered Gladstone bag in one hand, while delicately gripping the end

135

of his snow-white dhoti between the thumb and third finger of the other. He sprang up the steps with an elegance combined with authority.

'Where is the patient?' he asked briskly.

Prem Singh, the palms of his hands pressed together in a 'namaste', the Indian greeting, was edging before the doctor, indicating the way to Linda's room.

Mike stepped between them. 'I'll show you,' he said firmly, and led the doctor down the verandah.

Ronnie looked at Prem Singh and shrugged. Prem Singh beamed back at him, a smile brimming with amiability. 'Come,' he said warmly. 'Come and see my father. There is so much he wants to talk to you about.' He paused and looked over to the sleeping Ed. 'We leave him?'

'For the moment,' murmured Ronnie.

They wandered slowly across the compound. The heat was building up now, and shade was at a premium. Ram Singh's charpoy had been brought out and placed in the stripy shade of a clump of banana trees. Here, the old man lounged placidly smoking a cheroot and watching the women and children clustered round the water pump. He looked up eagerly as Ronnie approached.

'Welcome, welcome, Ronnieji!' he croaked, and shifted himself over on the wooden-framed bed to make room for Ronnie to sit. 'Has my son been taking good care of you?' he asked.

'Oh, yes, yes, and he has fetched Dr Prasad to see my mother.'

'Ah, yes, poor lady!' The old man sighed sympathetically. 'Europeans need time to adjust to India, yes? Now you, you have not been ill?'

'No, not at all,' said Ronnie. 'Touch wood!' He laughed.

'That's your Indian blood. It protects you!'

'I suppose so.' Ronnie spoke quietly, suddenly relaxing into the comfortable atmosphere of domestic sounds. They sat for a while without talking, watching the children splashing and squealing, the woman singing as she pummelled her washing, and the endless coo-cooing of the dove pigeon.

At last Ronnie said, 'Ram Singh, I must find my father. Henry Saville said my search should begin in the forest? How do I get there?'

The old man removed the cheroot from his mouth and gazed at him with a shaking head. 'My dear Ronnieji,' he murmured. 'The forest has gone. It went twenty years ago, soon after Henry Saville returned to England. Timber merchants came from the city and within a month they had cleared the forest. They left the villagers without fuel, the animals without shelter and even the river changed course and wandered off far away, so that the women have to walk miles to get water. No, Ronnie, the forest has gone. It is destroyed. You will not find it. The India of Henry Saville has gone.'

'Then what shall I do? Where shall I start? If my father found the same situation ten years ago, where would he have gone if he was looking for home?'

'Your father was not just looking for home. He was looking for Self. All those years he had been in bondage. The singing bowls taught him that, just as they are teaching you. He returned to India to find Self. Who was he in England? A brown Englishman? Henry Saville's son? No. His life was based on a falsity.'

'Was my grandfather, Henry Saville, wrong to adopt my father?'

'What is right? What is wrong? He had no choice. He did his duty. It was his obligation and no one else's. He knew that. He understood the importance of the bowls, so the link was kept. The truth was always there, waiting to be discovered. Even if your father had stayed here, he would have had to discover Self. We all do. Without that, how could he be a good husband or a good father? That is why he left you.'

'Truly, it is not because of the husband that the husband is loved, but because of Self.

And it is not because of the wife that the wife is loved, but because of Self.'

Ronnie spoke the words softly, remembering them in the one and only letter his father had sent his mother from India.

'Ahah!' The old man sighed fervently. 'You have been reading the Upanishads. And it is not because of the son that the son is loved, but because of Self.' The old man leaned forward and put a hand on his shoulder. 'Isn't that so, Ronnie?'

'Yes. I am beginning to understand,' Ronnie almost whispered. 'But . . .'

'Be patient. This is India. You have only just arrived. You must learn to find your rhythm in a new country. Give yourself time to feel and understand. Knowledge comes to us differently here. Henry Saville Sahib learned that in the forest. He learned it from your grandmother and your great-grandfather. You must learn it too.'

'Have I the time?' asked Ronnie with sudden impatience. 'I've only got three weeks. My grandfather was here a lifetime.'

'Start your search from the inside. Start with Self.' The old man's voice thickened with drowsiness.

'What am I supposed to do? Sit cross-legged and consider my navel?' Ronnie kicked the dust. 'There must be someone who knows.'

'You have the singing bowls. Listen to them.' He leaned forward with sudden intensity. 'After you played the bowls last night, did anything happen?'

'No. I don't think so.'

The old man studied him through half-closed eyes. 'Nothing? No one?'

'An American called Ed came. I met him on the train. He wanted to sleep on the verandah for the night. He's still there.'

'Ah!' The old man lay back on his bed. 'An American called Ed.' He cushioned his head in the fold of his elbow, and with a long sigh, drifted into sleep.

Ronnie walked slowly back across the compound, wondering.

Dr Prasad was still with Linda. His tonga waited, the little, bony horse rested on three legs, his fourth raised casually on the hoof; the tonga wallah lounged in the back of the tonga, smoking and chatting with the children.

Ronnie was going to see if Ed was awake, when Dr Prasad emerged with Mike. 'How's Mum?'

'She's OK. I think,' said Mike, frowning. He still looked worried. 'Dr Prasad says it might be a week or two before she's up on her feet.'

'A week or two?' Ronnie exclaimed with horror. 'But we're only in India for three weeks. What's wrong with her?'

'It is a virus. A stomach complaint,' explained Dr Prasad. 'We have so many in India – so many that we can't give them all names – or indeed have medicines for all of them. Time is the real physician. But I have given Mr Mike here a prescription for some pills. They will help her to keep down her food. She needs strength.'

'Prem Singh's taking me to the hospital to get them,' said Mike, and walked off quickly towards the servants' quarters.

The tonga wallah heaved himself over to the front of his carriage and took up the driving position with whip in hand. The horse resumed standing on four legs, and flicked the flies off his back with his tail. The doctor climbed aboard.

'Send for me any time you are worried, but otherwise, I will call again in a week.' He smiled at the sight of Ronnie's agonised expression. 'You must be patient.'

'We've come here to find my father. How can we now?' Suddenly, Ronnie gripped the side of the tonga. 'You knew Dr Bailey. He was the doctor here when my grandfather was District Commissioner. He looked after my father – the baby

Henry Saville adopted. Do you know about it? Has anyone come here who could have been my father?'

'So, you are Henry Saville's grandson – that baby's son, eh?' He looked at him compassionately. 'I don't know how to help you. I have heard nothing.'

'Is there anyone else left alive who knew Henry Saville?' asked Ronnie desperately. 'Where is Miss Murray, or Charlie, the dog catcher? Do you know them?'

Dr Prasad frowned. 'Charlie, the dog catcher. Yes, I knew him. He died some years ago. Miss Murray, now, she is alive, though very old and feeble. Still, her mind is clear. You could talk to her, though I doubt she knows anything.'

Ronnie felt a surge of excitement. 'Where is she? How do I find her?'

'She's in the Eventide Home. It's not far. In fact, if you like, come now in my tonga. I pass the place. Now would be a good time. She'll be awake.'

Ronnie pulled himself up into the seat next to the doctor. Once more he felt as though he was being drawn along by forces outside himself. Yet he also felt a chill presence. He was chasing old age; Henry Saville, Ram Singh, now Miss Murray. He had barely been one pace ahead of death, and death paced him now as he searched out the last of his grandfather's generation.

The bungalow receded as the horse sauntered through the opened gate and out into the wide, burning road. Ronnie felt a terrible sense of urgency, and was glad when the tonga wallah flicked his whip and the horse broke into a rapid trot.

18

FINDING MISS MURRAY

The Eventide Home shrank back almost apologetically from the main line of bungalows in Civil Lines, the old British residential area of Durgapur.

It had a pinched look about it; the grounds were not so generous, and except for a thin, parched tree at the gate, there were no other trees to provide shade and act as a foil to the heat of the sun.

The bungalow itself was built for economy and function, not for style, and the statement it made was one of last resort; those who were unfortunate enough not to have been able to return to England to die must retreat here.

To be fair, there had once been a broad, leafy hibiscus hedge. Its dusty remnants gasped in depleted clusters along what had been a boundary between the home and the much larger compound in which stood the once-proud Anglican church of All Souls. Scars of old. The flower-beds were also evidence of a more ordered and caring time, when old missionaries, unable or unwilling to let go of the India they had worked in for so long, ended their days behind the black and white shuttered windows, sustained by the Church and the rest of the British Community in something pertaining to an English style of life.

The church itself now was hardly more than a shell of its former self, echoing with emptiness, begging only that passing

visitors might read its plaque-covered walls testifying to generations of civil servants, soldiers, clergy and missionaries who
had lived and died, struggling with disease and uprisings and
the long journey home.

Thus was Ronnie dropped off on to this abandoned stage set,
and stood, an innocent at the gate, and read the rusty, metal
letters arched over the entrance, 'Eventide Home for the
Elderly'. The atmosphere was stultified, drug-like. Even the
ubiquitous chirp of the cricket was muted and intermittent. He
walked up the step to the nearest door. It was shut, and there
was no visible means by which to announce your arrival. He
walked round the verandah to the back. It was impossible to
peer inside through the closely-woven, wire-mesh windows.

. About twenty metres away were the low dwellings of the
servants' quarters. A woman sat on her haunches grinding
spices, but though the emaciated dog lying on the ground next
to her raised its head and barked belatedly at the arrival of a
stranger, she didn't look up, and no one came to investigate
who had come.

He saw another door. This one was ajar behind a half-
broken bamboo blind. Ronnie lifted the blind to one side and
called out. 'Hello! Is anyone there?' He waited. Listened.
Nothing. He stepped inside and called again. 'Hello!'

The gloom of the interior blinded him for a few moments,
and there was a heavy smell of latrines which made him feel
sick.

As his eyes adjusted, he saw that he stood in a smallish room
which must have served as a lobby. There was still an old oak
desk mouldering away at the side and riddled with beetle. A
dusty painting of George V stared down sternly from above the
mantelpiece. In a smaller alcove, and more endearing, was a
faded sampler, perhaps stitched by elderly fingers to pass the time
while waiting for death, 'Hitherto hath the Lord Delivered us.'

'Kansama! Kansama!' A quavery yet imperious voice called
out from somewhere deeper inside the bungalow. For a

moment, Ronnie fought the impulse to run and get away from this place as far as possible, but somehow, by the time he had reached the doorway and held back the broken blind, his courage returned to restrain him.

'Kansama? I know you're there. I heard you!'

'Excuse me!' Ronnie called apologetically through an intervening doorway.

'Who are you? Where's the kansama? I'm hungry,' continued the voice, apparently unperturbed by conversing with an intruder.

Ronnie followed the direction of the voice through the doorway, down an almost pitch dark passage and into another room of windowless gloom. Across this room he made out another doorway, this time graced by a faded, stripy, multicoloured curtain hanging by rings from a pole.

Ronnie lifted aside the curtain and immediately found himself face to face with the most ancient, old English woman he had ever seen. She was sitting bolt upright in bed, staring out with violet blue eyes set in a small round, shrunken face with skin like fine, but crumpled, white tissue paper.

'Have you seen the kansama?' she demanded. 'The man's late again. I don't know what's wrong with servants these days. Trouble is, there's no one to train them. Now, in my day . . .'

'Are you Miss Murray?' Ronnie interrupted.

'Yes, I am. What's it to you, young man?' She didn't wait for an answer. 'Do you know where the kansama is?'

'No, sorry!' Ronnie held out his hands apologetically. 'Who is the kansama?'

'The cook, of course.' She cocked her head on one side. 'What kind of person are you that you don't know that? Are you English or something. You don't look it, but you speak it. Who are you?'

'Ronnie Saville. You knew my grandfather. He was Henry Saville, the Assistant District Commissioner. You didn't want him to adopt the baby. Do you remember? It had smallpox and

143

was brought to him by an old woman? Well, he did adopt it, and took it to England. The baby was my father.'

'Good heavens! The saints preserve us!' The old woman looked at him with blue eyes sharpening to needles as her memory came flooding back.

'Yes, I told him it was ridiculous to take the child to England. I would have cared for it perfectly adequately in the orphanage. Quite misguided of him, it was ... and you?' she clasped her thin, white hands before her. 'You are the son of that baby?'

Ronnie nodded.

'Are you ... Did he?' her voice trailed, uncertain how to continue.

'Did it work out, you mean?' Ronnie helped her out. 'Kind of. But ten years ago my father left us and came back to India. He didn't tell us where. For a long time we didn't know if he was alive or dead. Now we're sure he's alive, and I want to find him. That's why I'm here. I thought he might start in Durgapur, as I have done. It was here he was adopted. His life really began here. Please, Miss Murray.'

'Henry Saville. Stubborn man. Is he still alive?'

Ronnie shook his head. 'No. He died three months ago.'

'Oh.' She sighed and sagged a little back into her pillows. 'I must be one of the few left from those days.' She closed her eyes.

'Miss Murray!' Ronnie spoke with sharp urgency. 'Has anyone been to see you – someone a bit like me? Maybe ten years ago? Someone who could have been my father?'

'No, no!' She answered emphatically without opening her eyes. 'Anyway, why should he want to see me? I couldn't help him. Now be a dear and find that wretched kansama for me. He's out there somewhere, probably eating my tiffin, the villain. Oh, servants, these days ...' she waved a hand dismissively.

Biting his lip with disappointment, Ronnie left the bedroom. He made his way out into the compound and walked towards the low corrugated-roofed dwellings.

144

The woman sitting on her haunches grinding spices was still there, as was the dog. Only when he called out, 'Kansama!' did she look up. 'Kansama!' repeated Ronnie more energetically, encouraged by the response.

The woman raised her head and shouted harshly in the direction of one of the huts. '*Garsum! Eh Garsum! Idder Aow!*'

A thin, languid man appeared in a doorway. He wandered out unhurriedly. 'Kansama!' Ronnie managed to add authority to his call, and pointed vigorously towards the bungalow.

With a look of sudden enlightenment, the man nodded cheerfully and disappeared into the hut. After a while he emerged carrying a stack of interlocking metal dishes and came towards the bungalow.

Ronnie didn't wait any further but returned quickly to Miss Murray.

This time he drew the cotton curtain aside more discreetly. Miss Murray lay with her head tipped right back so that her thin, veined throat lay exposed as if for execution.

'Miss Murray?' Ronnie spoke quietly but clearly.

She opened her eyes and again he was startled by how blue they were. 'Kansama?'

'He's coming. I found him', Ronnie assured her.

'Oh, it's you.' She heaved herself up. 'Help me with these pillows!' she ordered. Ronnie obediently settled the pillows behind her so that she was in a more upright position to receive her meal.

'I'd better go now,' said Ronnie, backing towards the doorway, 'unless there's anything you can tell me at all which might help?'

The kansama came in, impeding Ronnie's exit. He took the metal dishes to a side table and began to arrange the food on to a white, heavy-duty dinner plate. He then put the plate on to a tray and brought it to her lap. Throughout this procedure, Miss Murray spoke to him in Hindi, obviously words of chastisement, for she then broke into English and continued her criticisms for Ronnie's benefit.

'He'll let me starve to death one of these days, and he wouldn't care. There's no one to care. It'll be better when I'm dead.'

'Goodbye, Miss Murray,' said Ronnie edging closer to the curtain.

She had been combing through her food with a fork as if looking for foreign bodies. 'Can't find a decent cook these days. Look at this gristly meat and water-thin dhal. He's probably kept the best for himself. You can't trust servants, you know . . .'

'Yes,' sympathised Ronnie. 'I must go. Goodbye, Miss Murray.' He went through and the curtain dropped behind him.

'Hey you, Master Saville!' Her voice commanded him back.

He drew back the curtain. 'Yes?'

'I remember old Charlie, the dog catcher. He was in here with me – oh, many years back. Yes, he said some character had come to see him. Charlie was excited about it because the man brought some kind of bowl with him. Charlie called it a singing bowl. He could have sworn it was like one of the ones Henry Saville had.'

Ronnie was back at her bedside in one stride. 'Yes? Yes, Miss Murray? What else?' He had a terrible desire to shake her, as if somehow it would shake all her memories out of her head.

'There was something else. The man was dressed like a sadhu, a holy man. He had beads and things and . . . his hair was long and matted . . . and . . . yes, there was one very strange thing, Charlie said,' she paused and gave a high quavery laugh. 'This sadhu spoke like an English public schoolboy, would you believe it?'

'Yes,' murmured Ronnie. 'I would believe it, because he was an English public schoolboy. What else?' He spoke now almost like a counsel in court questioning a witness.

'What else?' She sighed, as though her memories weighed heavily.

'He seemed to know about Charlie. He knew that Charlie had some knowledge about singing bowls. Charlie was old

146

then, you know. His mind was going a bit. He told me about this visit, because it bothered him. He was trying to remember what it was about this singing bowl because, of course, you never see them round here, Charlie told me. They're not Indian, you know, they're Tibetan. Must have come across the border with traders. Charlie had forgotten that he had explained about singing bowls to Henry Saville. He got his with the baby . . . yes . . .' She paused and looked up at Ronnie. 'Did you say you were the baby?'

'No, no. My father was. I'm looking for him. What else did Charlie say? There must have been something else? Please . . .' He stopped himself in time from saying, 'Please don't get muddled.'

'There was nothing else,' she cackled again. 'A sadhu with an English public-school accent! What a thought!' When she had finished laughing she said, 'There was one other thing . . . I can't remember his exact words.' She closed her eyes. The fork slid from her fingers into the dhal. Ronnie retrieved it and wiped it, barely taking his eyes off her.

She opened her eyes. They were still laughing. 'Did you ever . . .?'

'Yes?' asked Ronnie, with supreme patience.

'Did you ever hear of the pilgrim's route? That's what Charlie mentioned. Charlie told him that if he followed the pilgrim's route up to the mountains, the Himalayas, he'd find out more about that bowl. That's it. Now, young man, I must eat my food.' She picked up her fork.

'Call again sometime, won't you.'

Thus, tersely dismissed, Ronnie muttered 'goodbye' and left.

Once outside, he wandered along the roadside in a dream. For a while he didn't notice or care where he was going. All he could think of was that at last he had met someone who had news of his father. And now too, he had another lead. The pilgrim's route. Who would know about that? Ram Singh? Ronnie walked faster.

He became aware of his surroundings, and managed to remember the route back to Henry's bungalow.

The compound was deserted. Ed's rucksack and sleeping bag had all gone. There was no sign he had even been there. With a feeling of unease, he hurried along to Linda's room. She was there. He heaved a sigh of relief. She was sleeping peacefully, the fan above her head whirring gently, ruffling her hair and drying the perspiration which would have otherwise gathered on her brow.

He still felt uneasy. The place seemed too quiet. He went to his room. He would take the singing bowls to Ram Singh and question him about the pilgrim's route to the mountains.

He reached into the closet where he had stored the bowls this morning. He found one, and set it on the table. He felt for the other. Nothing. He scrabbled round with an increasing sense of panic. Where was the other? The closet was empty. He looked in the drawers, under the bed, on top of the closet, under his pillows – he looked when he saw there was no point in looking. He knew with a numbing horror, it had gone.

'Ed!' he shouted wildly. 'Ed!' It had to be Ed. 'You shit!' He was overwhelmed with fury. He rushed out of the bungalow towards the servants' quarters. Ram Singh was lying on his charpoy surrounded by elders and drinking tea.

Ronnie ignored them all. He held out the last singing bowl for Ram Singh to see. 'The American, Ed! He's gone. He's stolen one of the bowls. You didn't expect that, did you?' He flung himself down on his knees by the bed.

Prem Singh came over to the group. 'Didn't I tell you,' he said. 'These hippies are the worst.'

19
GOING IT ALONE

'Start with Self,' Ram Singh had said. But where was Self? Who was Self? Who could tell him?

Ronnie walked slowly back towards the bungalow. Anger and bewilderment flooded over him in alternate waves. He held the last remaining bowl clutched tightly to his chest, his finger tips kneading the metal. 'You bastard, Ed!' he whimpered. 'Start with Self. Start with Self. How can I when I don't know who I am?' His breath echoed round the dark interior of the bowl.

He reached the dark circle of shade of the tamarind tree and stepped inside. Before him, the driveway stretched on and on towards the gate. The gate seemed a long way off, and as he mused over this, the sky darkened. A great silence descended. The birds stopped singing, and the voices from across the grounds faded away. The sun became the moon and a million pinpricks of light became stars. The day became night.

Out of the darkness, a figure came slowly walking. It was a tall upright man, an opaque shape made almost invisible in the gloom, except when a sudden puff on the pipe revealed the profile of a face in the scarlet glow of tobacco.

'Grandpa!' Ronnie reached out. 'Wait for me!'

'Where the hell have you been!'

Like a sleepwalker roughly awakened, Ronnie jolted. Night became day.

'Your mother's been asking for you. Why did you leave the compound?'

Mike stood on the verandah, his arms folded and his feet apart. 'I wanted you to keep her company while I went with Ram Singh to get some money changed at the bank.'

Ronnie approached and nodded towards the empty corner on the verandah. 'So you got rid of him after all.'

'Didn't need to,' Mike answered smoothly. 'He got rid of himself. Got the message.'

Yes, Ronnie could see how Ed got the message. It was outlined in Mike's body, it was written across his face.

Ronnie went to Linda's room. Mike followed.

'Ronnie!' There were tears in her voice as she sat up with relief. 'I was worried. Mike said you weren't to be found. Luckily one of Prem Singh's children saw you go with the doctor in the tonga. You should have told us. Where did you go?'

He described his visit to Miss Murray. He told her about the holy man who came to visit Charlie, the dog catcher. The holy man with the public-school accent.

'You mean . . . Adam did come here? Was it Adam?'

Concern, pleasure, expectancy, fear; Ronnie saw all those expressions fleet across her face. She looked from Ronnie to Mike. He had seen them too. He turned his back and stared out of the doorway across the compound.

'That's all she could tell me,' Ronnie ended softly, 'and it was years ago. Dad could be anywhere now.'

Linda lay back on her pillows, her face now expressionless, her feelings internalised. For a long while she fixed her eyes on the whirring fan above her head. Then she murmured, 'So what are we going to do? Where do we go from here?'

'Nowhere!' Mike wheeled round forthrightly and strode over to the bed. He gathered her up in his arms and pressed his

150

face to hers. 'We're going nowhere, except home. It's obviously a hopeless task. I knew so all along. Look! Now that we know, you get better, and if we've time left, let's go and see a few of the sights. The Taj Mahal, or some of the temples we've heard about. He's gone, Linda. Adam's gone out of your life for good. You know it now. He doesn't want to be found. Forget him.'

'Ronnie?' Linda shook herself free of Mike. She had heard her son leave. 'Ronnie!'

'He'll get over it.' Mike clasped her again. Willing her to see things his way. 'I'll get Prem Singh to take him round on the motorbike. He'll soon put the whole thing out of his mind. He can see it's useless. Linda! Look at me.' He held her face fiercely. If he could, he would have ripped out the part of her brain that thought of anyone else. He made her look at him. 'I want to marry you. Forget that bloody man and this bloody country. You're divorced from Adam now. Divorce yourself from his memory too, and his spirit. Let's get on with living, you and me. Please. I love you, Linda.'

They had supper together that evening, all three of them. Linda in bed; Mike and Ronnie sitting at a table nearby which Prem Singh had brought in for them.

It was subdued meal; each thoughtful and low-voiced, as if much of importance had been expressed and much needed evaluation.

When they had eaten, Mike went outside on the verandah to smoke. Ronnie and Linda eyed each other silently for a while, then Ronnie spoke.

'Mum, don't worry. Whatever happens on this trip, don't worry, especially about me, Concentrate on getting better, and concentrate on sorting out your feelings for Mike. I just don't want you to make a mistake about him. Be sure, Mum. Be sure you really want to marry him.' His voice trailed away. 'That's all! Whatever you decide, I'm on your side. OK?'

'Ronnie!' Linda cried out his name. It hung in the air, her thought unsaid. Then she murmured, 'You've changed, you

151

know. Since coming to India, in just three days, you seem to have changed, almost overnight. You've grown-up.' She sounded sad.

Ronnie nodded. 'Yes. Well, I'm able to look after myself. That's why I don't want you worrying about me. It doesn't matter whether Mike and I get on. We don't have to. All that matters is that you are happy.' Ronnie got to his feet and made for the door. 'Grandpa was right. He said you were still young, and that I should understand. I do now. Bye, Mum! Just get well and don't worry.' Then he was gone.

Later, she would say that she knew it was a farewell. Later, she would remember in detail every word, every phrase and every expression. 'Bye, Mum! Just get well and don't worry.' She would remember that he said 'goodbye' and not 'good-night'.

Ronnie, too, would remember his goodbye many, many times over in the days that followed. There had been no other way. Mike was draining them all of the will to carry on the search. He had to go alone.

He left Henry Saville's bungalow that night with just his rucksack on his shoulder and the singing bowl tucked at the top of it. He walked up the drive past the tamarind tree, invisible in the darkness, and though shadowy figures moved across the compound, and the old chowkidar puffed on his hookah near the gate, no one acknowledged him, and like a ghost, he seemed to pass unseen on to the road outside.

He automatically turned left and followed the road, running broad and tree-lined through the old British neighbourhood. The feeling of invisibility continued; even when he hit the raucous glare of the bazaar, no one took any notice of him pushing his way on and on through the jostling crowds.

He suddenly found himself standing before the grain shop where he had been taken after being thrown from Prem Singh's motorbike. It was no surprise to him to find himself

152

there. Somehow he knew, if a little after the fact, that he had intended that all along.

The holy man was sitting in the tea shop opposite.

Ronnie crossed the road and went over to the stone verandah which rose above an overflowing gutter at the side. The holy man sat on a rickety bench lounging over an old wooden table, his hands cupped round a metal bowl of steaming tea. He didn't look at Ronnie as he approached, though Ronnie knew he was aware of his presence.

A kerosene lamp hanging from an awning, quivered slightly, sending ripples of shadows across the faces. The tea-shop man boiled his water in old, discarded paraffin tins. He mixed and poured, mixed and poured concoctions of water, milk, tea, sugar and spices, stirring and brewing like an old magician. He caught Ronnie's eye. 'Tea?' He read the silent question.

Ronnie nodded his silent reply. The tea-shop man went into his final phase of tea-making, cooling the mixture, by pouring it at arm's length from one paraffin can to another. The liquid flowed like a piece of silk falling a metre at a time and then tipped, at last into a round metal bowl.

Ronnie climbed the verandah steps and exchanged a rupee for the bowl of tea, then he retreated down the steps again to perch respectfully below the holy man.

The holy man still studiously avoided his eye. Ronnie sipped his tea for a while. He felt calm and untroubled. He was finding a rhythm. There was time enough. He had nearly drunk the full bowl of tea when the holy man stretched his body out across the bench. Ronnie was afraid he was settling down to sleep. He quickly undid his rucksack and took out the singing bowl. Then mounting the steps once more, placed it on the table in front of the holy man.

'Where must I go to find those who understand the language of singing bowls?' he asked.

The effect was immediate. The holy man sat up violently and drew his legs beneath him, recoiling from the bowl.

153

Ronnie thought the singing bowl looked almost common-place, standing as it did alongside the tea bowls on the table. It looked less polished and shiny, its metal not so smooth, nor its shape so even as the other bowls. Compared to the others it looked crude, even ugly.

They stared at it, the tea man from his dark, steaming corner, the holy man cringing away on the bench, and Ronnie standing, persistently, at the table.

Then tentatively, the holy man stretched out a hand and slowly pulled the bowl towards him. He withdrew his hand and examined the bowl closely, looking through narrowed eyes. He stretched his hand out again and this time lifted the bowl towards his lips. Then, instead of running a finger round the rim as Ronnie had always done, the holy man blew across the top through pursed lips.

At first they heard nothing but his breath striking against empty air, but he kept blowing and blowing, altering the shape of his lips and the angle at which he blew. Then suddenly, they heard it. A low sound, almost like a human sigh, such as Ronnie had never heard before.

The tea-shop man stood up clasping his hands anxiously, and came over to the table muttering, '*Ram, Ram!*'

The holy man continued blowing. The sound increased from a sighing to a moaning, so deep and so troubled. Now after he had blown his breath across the rim, the holy man ran his finger round and round, helping to perpetuate the sound, causing it to rise and fall in menacing waves.

'*Bus, bus bhai*! Stop! begged the tea man. He reached over and snatched the bowl from the holy man and thrust it at Ronnie.

'Go,' he cried angrily. 'Go! Take it away.'

'Just tell me where I must go, please!' Ronnie entreated. The holy man stared at him with eyes returning to consciousness.

'You told me I was searching, do you remember?' Ronnie challenged him. 'You also told me I would find. My search is bound up with this bowl. I must know where to start. Tell me.'

The holy man looked angry and agitated. 'You have no right to such a bowl,' he cried. 'They are sacred and the property of holy men and temples. In the wrong hands, these bowls are dangerous. They speak, they sing, they address spirits, but they also summon up demons and evil powers. Tormented souls get trapped inside their shapes. Only people with knowledge should touch these bowls. Who knows what spirits I have released just now.' He got up, looking frightened. 'Take it away. You would do better to throw it into the river than attempt to find out its secrets. Go, Go!' He waved his arm furiously. 'Go to the station. Go with the pilgrims. There are trains going north towards the mountains where the gods dwell. But do not take the bowl. Only evil will come of it.'

The tea man was now pushing Ronnie down the steps. 'Go. Leave us,' he shouted roughly.

Ronnie stumbled into the road, the bowl clasped in his arms. How could it be evil? It had belonged to his father and grandfather before him. Henry never spoke of it being evil. No, the bowl was part of him. He knelt down in the dust with the crowd swirling indifferently around him, and defiantly thrust the bowl back into his rucksack.

He felt the eyes of the tea man and the holy man burning into his back, but he didn't look round. Heaving the rucksack on to his back he strode off towards the station. Good or Evil, the bowl was his only hope of finding his father, and if that meant a train going north, then that was where he would go.

20
DEEPAK TAKES HIM NORTH

Ronnie crouched in the open doorway of the train as it extricated itself from the station. It was nearly dawn. He had spent the night on the station platform. Despite the heat, he had burrowed down into his sleeping bag trying to block off the noise, smells and discomfort, but to no avail; and when the ancient, blackened steam train came hissing and grinding into the station, it was with a feeling of sleepless despair that he allowed himself to be swept on board by the multitude. The whole world, it seemed, wanted to travel north.

For the first time since leaving Henry's bungalow, Ronnie was racked with indecision and uncertainty. He had forgotten why he was doing what he was doing and where he thought he was going. For the first time, he felt really alone and he didn't know how he was going to manage . . . He had thrown himself on the mercy of India.

The train was bursting with people; the compartments, the corridors, and even on the outside of the train, people clung precariously to footholds, and ledges, or sprawled across the roof.

At least where he crouched, tightly hemmed into his own tiny space, Ronnie could be grateful for being near the open door. The worst that could happen was that he would tumble out due to the pressure of people behind him. But at this moment, such a fate seemed to be the least of his problems.

'Start with Self.' He heard again, Ram Singh's voice. 'Self, Self, Self!' Ronnie exploded to himself bitterly. 'Well, here I am, Self. Tell me what to do.'

He wondered what Ed was doing. Had his stolen bowl led him northwards, too? Anger swept over him. 'You bastard, you bastard!' he wept inwardly. 'You thief, you traitor! Why couldn't you have waited for me?' He bowed his head into his hands.

The train siren screamed a shrill double note. The old steam engine, hissing and puffing at last, found its rhythm and broke into a gallop across the burning, Indian plain.

As the train settled down, so too did the people, surrendering themselves to the mesmeric passing of time.

Hours later the train stopped briefly at a small, dusty station. It was empty except for a few scavenging crows, and some mangey dogs, too starved to do more than raise an eye, which noted that no one got off, except the guard.

The only vendor to be seen was an old peanut-seller and his boy. The boy carried on his head a large, matted tray piled high with a mountain of peanuts. The old man's tenor and the young boy's shrill soprano, called in counterpoint up the platform. Neither could move very fast; the old man, because he was old and lame, and the young boy because he was so weighed down with the huge tray on his head.

Ronnie peered out of the doorway. He watched them slowly working their way up the train. He felt a lurching pang of hunger and fumbled in his pocket for some annas. But just then, the whistle blew, the guard jumped back on the train, as with a great hissing and shuddering, it moved off once more.

Ronnie sat back weakly, cursing his slowness of action.

The notion of food was catching. A flurry of movement stirred his fellow passengers. Children looked up expectantly and old men smacked their lips. Bundles were unfastened, tin boxes opened, and smells which had been trapped in every kind of container and wrapping were now released into the air. Chapattis, pooris, vegetable curry and pakoras, all were passed from hand to hand round family groups, making Ronnie feel so unbearably hungry that it took all he had, to resist the temptation of holding out his hand like a beggar.

Distantly, far down the corridor and round the corner into the next, Ronnie heard the treble cry of the peanut-seller's boy. He must have boarded the train. He fumbled for his annas, then waited with mounting expectation, for the peanuts to come his way.

Now the cry was nearer. Now Ronnie could see the great, round tray, disembodied from its owner, appearing to bob over a sea of heads, floating steadily towards him.

At last Ronnie held out his annas. 'Peanuts!' he cried.

The tray stopped dead still, and quivered. 'Ron-ee? Ron-ee?' The boy's voice rose even higher with excitement. 'Is that you?'

Amazed at hearing his name, Ronnie peered under the rim of the tray, and there beaming up at him, grinning a grin so wide that it exposed every tooth in his head, was Deepak!

To see a familiar face, a friendly face, at a time when he was feeling most desolate, caused a rush of tears to mingle with his astounded laughter.

'What the bloody hell are you doing here?' cried Ronnie.

'Me? Bloody hell. Me helping sell peanuts for the old man. He's getting too old. He looked after me once. Now I look after him. Without me, he'd starve.' They stared at each other with mutual pleasure, then Deepak said, 'I go up train. Sell more peanuts and come back.' He began to move on his way.

'Hang on, Deepak. Don't go before you've sold me some, please. I'm starving!'

'Poor Ron-ee!' cried Deepak with mock tragedy. He twisted a torn page of printed paper into a cone shape, reached up for a handful of peanuts and dropped them in.

'Thanks, mate!' Ronnie immediately tossed a palmful down his throat as Deepak's high call 'Peanuts!' drifted away down the next corridor.

It was an hour at least before Deepak returned. He was without the cumbersome tray which he said he had left further up under the eye of the guard. But he hadn't returned empty-handed; his turban was filled with peanuts for Ronnie.

For a while they sat in companionable silence, cracking nuts and tossing the shells out into the slowly passing countryside.

'Where mother? Where Mike?' Deepak finally asked.

I've left them in Durgapur. My mother was too ill to travel, so I came on alone.'

'Still looking for father?'

'Yes.' Ronnie tossed some shells on to the side of the track. 'Deepak?' He glanced at the ragged boy who sat at his side. 'How come you speak such good English?'

Deepak didn't answer at once. He looked guarded; wary. Then he said, 'You search for father. I search for mother. I know that my father is dead, but my mother . . .' he shook his head.

'What happened? Where is she?' asked Ronnie.

'The last time I saw her, she was in the flower market in the city. We had gone there to choose garlands for a big *puja* that was taking place. A holy day to celebrate the goddess Sarasvatti. We lived in a big house. My father was a business man before he died. I went to an English-speaking school. That is where I learned English, and many of my father's friends spoke English. I was young, only about six years old.'

'What happened in the market?' asked Ronnie.

'I was standing with my back to a stone pillar. It was cool, and I remember the smell of the tube lilies and the roses. There were mountains of flowers and garlands. I was sure that Heaven must be like that. My mother was bending over, talking to the flower-seller, carefully selecting the flowers she wanted, when suddenly, this beautiful lady in a shining, green

159

saree came up to me. She smiled so sweetly, as if she knew me. She said she had something very special to show me. She took my hand – not roughly – but like a friend and led me away towards a large, black car which was parked nearby. There was a man inside. He looked friendly, too. He opened the door and said, "Come in here and just look at these toys." He had some models of cars, all of different colours. They did look nice. I got inside. The car drove off. I felt worried about my mother but at first they reassured me and said she knew where I had gone and that they were friends of hers. Later, I cried. They left me alone for a long, long time. At last, an old woman came with some food. I wept bitterly. I told her I wanted to go home to my mother. The old woman said, "Stop snivelling, child. You will never see your mother again." '

'And did you?' asked Ronnie with quiet horror.

'No. I go to the flower market, and I look at all the ladies buying flowers, bending over so carefully, selecting as my mother did. She was always so particular, and I think "could one of those ladies be her?" Sometimes I stand in front of them, make sure they see my face. Surely, she would recognise her own son, wouldn't she?'

'I don't know. You must be so changed!' Ronnie shook his head, appalled at Deepak's story. 'What did they do with you? What has happened to you all these years?'

'These child kidnappers, they are the worst. They have no pity. They would have chopped off an arm or one of my legs so that I would be such a pitiful beggar, people would give me lots of money. But when they realised I spoke good English, the woman said, "Don't maim him. We can train him to be a good thief. We will set him on to the tourists. Take him to Delhi and Bombay, to Agra and Jaipur." I tell you, Ronnie, there is not one pocket, purse, suitcase or rucksack that is safe with me. I steal money, passports, air tickets, train tickets, travellers cheques, watches – everything and anything,' he ended bitterly.

'But you didn't steal from us,' commented Ronnie.

'No, last year, somehow – perhaps one of the children risked his life and went to the police, but the people were arrested. The whole syndicate collapsed.'

'But that's great!' cried Ronnie. 'Couldn't the police help you to find your mother again?'

'You must be mad! Do you think I would have gone anywhere near the police? They would have thrown me into prison, too. After all, I have been a thief for the past six years. No! We all ran away. But I said to myself, God has given me a chance. I must be the sort of person my mother would wish me to be, then perhaps I will be rewarded, and we will find each other. I swear to you, Ronnie. I am not a thief any more. You are safe with me.'

The heat of the day seared into the doorway of the train. For the boys, there was no escape, trapped as they were by the pressure of bodies behind them.

Ronnie's head ached and his limbs stiffened with fatigue. The sun burned into his face, closing his eyes with its glare. From time to time he slipped into momentary sleep, only to jerk awake just in time to stop himself from tumbling from the train.

The train slowed down almost to a walking pace. In the near distance, a patch of water gasped for existence within the arid bed of a river run almost dry. 'Come, Ronnie. Jump off here. There are still three more hours before we reach a station. You will fall off the train before then. Besides, aren't you thirsty? I am.' He tugged at his sleeve. 'Jump now, while the train is slow.'

Ronnie wanted to protest. He wanted to cry out, 'I must go on. I haven't much time,' but he was thirsty. His head throbbed, and his mouth felt too swollen to form any words. He nodded feebly.

Deepak jumped first. Rather, swung down, hanging briefly from the pole, his feet barely a centimetre from the ground. Then dropping on to the track without stumbling.

Ronnie struggled with his rucksack.

'Throw it, Ronnie, throw it!' cried Deepak jogging alongside the train with his arms outstretched.

The train was beginning to gather speed. 'Hurry! Throw me the rucksack and get off!' urged Deepak.

At last, Ronnie tossed the rucksack down to the boy, and immediately followed, clumsily, so that he fell and rolled on the sharp chippings.

'What about your peanuts?' was all Ronnie could mutter, as Deepak knelt anxiously beside him.

'You OK, Ronnie?'

Ronnie nodded speechlessly. Deepak tugged him to his feet. 'Let's get to the river. Then we'll be all right,' he said.

It had been a river once, even the most ancient of dried-up river beds leave their courses stamped into the earth. This was the slightest trickle of water, fumbling among large, dusty boulders; disappearing at times into the cracked earth, then re-emerging at gentle slopes to fall into some semblance of a pool.

It turned Ronnie and Deepak into children. They kicked and splashed and sprayed each other, and wallowed and gulped, and then crawled away to fall exhausted but tingling, into the slight, fragmented shade of a thorn bush.

He hadn't thought about the bowl until then. He hadn't wanted to think about the bowl. What had happened in the tea shop had disturbed him more profoundly than he cared to realise.

He glanced at Deepak. The boy had fallen into the instant sleep of a child, one arm slung across his face as a shield, the other outstretched on the hot, brown earth.

Ronnie took the bowl from his rucksack and moved down the river bed. When he had gone some three hundred metres, he stopped among a jumble of boulders. He placed the bowl on

162

one of them whose surface was flattened out like a table, then he sat back and studied it.

So they didn't just sing, these bowls, they spoke, too. They contained powers, spirits, demons. He remembered the holy man and how afraid he had been. The fear was real. It might all be stupid superstition, but they believed it, and when you believe, other powers come into force.

He picked up the bowl and held it to his mouth as the holy man had done. He blew across the rim, but produced no sound. For a few minutes, he tried vainly, blowing at different angles, altering the shape of his lips, blowing harder, softer, with his tongue or without, but nothing happened. He put the bowl down again and ran his finger round the rim. Now he produced a sound, as before. A low, humming, throbbing sound which he controlled by the pressure and speed of his finger. He allowed the hum to build up so that the whole bowl vibrated, then he bent down till his lips were level with the rim, and he blew.

The bowl clattered on the rock, almost bouncing up and down with the intensity of sound which shook it. Excitedly, Ronnie went on blowing, pressing his lips to the bowl's rim as if it were a flute. Now the reverberations spread through his lips and cheeks and into the very bone structure of his face. It seemed to fill the cavities of his skull and make the tissues of his brain quiver.

There was a voice. He could hear it. It sounded like a voice trying to shout under water, muffled but intense. He continued the blowing, though the blood rushed into his head, blurred his eyes and made him sway with dizziness. The voice got louder. It was shouting a word, but he couldn't make it out. He picked up the bowl now and had it clutched to his mouth. He blew and blew, rocking to and fro on his heels, trapped by its rhythm, hypnotised by the searing notes, obsessed by the voice, now accompanied by other voices who all seemed to be calling to him, beseeching him.

Behind him, Deepak awoke with a shriek, shuddering with a chill which had gripped his limbs, though the sun still burned hot in the sky.

'Ronnie! Ronnie!'

Ronnie was moaning and swaying. Deepak stumbled towards him. At last the bowl fell from Ronnie's exhausted hands, and as Deepak reached him he slumped over a rock, his shoulders heaving, his breaths coming out in painful gasps.

'Ronnie! What is happening! I don't understand. Was it all a dream?' Deepak clutched his arm and felt his brow. 'Are you ill, Ronnie?' He bent down and grasped the fallen bowl. He raced over to the trickle of water, filled the bowl and brought it back.

'Here, drink, drink!' Ronnie drank, tipping the bowl up till every drop was drained from it. Again, Deepak went to fill the bowl. This time, when he returned, Ronnie was sitting on the ground, holding his head in his hands. He drank again.

Deepak crouched near him. His body still shivered. 'I had a dream.' His voice trembled. 'It was so vivid. It was so real. I was in a flower market watching a lady bending down choosing flowers. It was my mother. I knew it was she, and I was waiting for her to get up and turn round. Suddenly, I heard a voice calling. I turned to see who it was, and when I looked again, my mother had vanished. The voice went on calling, "Come, come!" I went into the bazaar, down narrow alleyways, right into the poorest part of the town. The voice kept calling and calling. It led me into a crumbling house, dark and smelling foul. I climbed narrow, broken stairs and then I came to a room. It was completely bare. It had one tiny grille for a window, and the walls and floorboards were rotting and festooned with cobwebs.'

Deepak paused, as if trying to remember with greater clarity. 'There was a man in the room, curled up in a corner as if he was ill. He was a Westerner, wearing jeans and T-shirt, like so many of those hippy types you see round the cities. He was rocking and moaning to himself. Before him, on the floor, was a bowl. Like this one, Ronnie. Just a simple bowl, yet in my dream, it seemed to be growing bigger and bigger until I was afraid.'

Ronnie got to his feet. 'Ed!' he murmured.

'Ed?' Deepak looked puzzled.

'What else, Deepak?' asked Ronnie urgently. 'What else was in your dream? What happened then?'

'Nothing. I woke up. Someone seemed to be screaming. I don't know if it was in my dream, or . . .' he paused and looked anxiously at Ronnie, 'or if it was you?' Ronnie didn't answer. They walked slowly back along the river bed towards the thorn bushes.

'Are you sure there was nothing else in your dream? Nothing to tell you where this town was? The bazaar, the house?'

'No!' Deepak shook his head, frowning with concentration, as he racked his memory of the dream. 'Except!'

Ronnie stopped dead. 'Except what?'

'A holy man. There was a holy man. I passed him at the bottom of the stairs in the house. He was going out.'

'What did he look like?'

'As all holy men look. He had a bowl like yours.'

'Ah!' Ronnie nodded. 'You have seen my father before I have.'

Deepak looked at Ronnie in amazement, but did not attempt to ask any questions. Ronnie had such a strange and private expression on his face.

When Ronnie had put away the bowl he stood up and stared into the far distance. 'Look at that long line of white clouds on the horizon,' he said. 'They are the first clouds I have seen in India.'

'No, Ronnie! Those are not clouds,' said Deepak. 'They are the mountains of everlasting snows. You are looking at the Himalayas!'

After a while, they heard the shriek of a train whistle in the distance.

Shyly, Deepak touched Ronnie's arm. 'We must go, Ronnie. We must catch this train or spend the night outside.'

'Will the train take us closer to the mountains?' asked Ronnie. 'Is it a train going north?'

'Yes. By morning you will have to lift your head backwards to see the peaks of the mountains rising before you.'

'Then all is well,' said Ronnie.

The two boys walked swiftly towards the railway track.

21

AN ENCOUNTER
WITH SELF

Ronnie slept. He slept the sleep of the vagrant; lolling in some corner of a train corridor, shifting along when his space became unviable, lying in positions not associated with sleep, his head thrown back, his limbs twisted unnaturally, his heart fluttering with fatigue; only sleeping because a body has to sleep in the end, no matter what.

He slept the sleep of the hungry; as if a rat had gnawed its way into his entrails, consuming him from the inside, tearing at his guts, tugging at the fibres of his muscles, so that he moaned fitfully, clasping his arms around himself for comfort, curling into a foetal position as if he could somehow return to the comfort of the womb.

Most of all, he slept the sleep of the ignorant. If only he had known that the blur of white horizon which he had taken for clouds, were not just the everlasting snows that Deepak had told him about, not just the Himalayas, a name on an atlas, but that what he had glimpsed was the dwelling place of the gods; that for millions of Hindus right across Asia, the Himalayas were the centre of the universe.

If only he had known, his hunger would have been forgotten. Instead, his mind and soul would have been reaching out, travelling ahead of himself up the soft, flowery paths, up the wooded slopes of the foothills; higher into the pine forests riven with steep gulleys and treacherous ravines, where precipices plunge a thousand feet and icy rivers hurl themselves from their glacial sources, to rush down on to the thirsty plains below; up and up through mountain passes, following the tracks of traders and tribal horsemen, into the white, snow-blinding realms of ice and rocks, where mountain peaks, sharp as tiger's teeth bare their ferocity to the skies.

Only when the clattering and chattering, hissing and whistling had finally ceased, when all motion was stilled and the opened doors let in a rush of sweet air, only then did Ronnie stir into semi-wakefulness, dully opening and shutting his eyes as he struggled for consciousness.

He attempted to stand up, but waves of nausea, dizziness and hunger swept the strength from his limbs and tipped him into a sea of darkness.

'Ronnie! Ronnie! Get up. We have arrived at the foot of the mountains. The train can go no further!' He felt Deepak's thin arms trying to heave him to his feet.

Mechanically, Ronnie's limbs went into motion, and he allowed Deepak to lead him, like a sleepwalker, away from the station and out into the town.

He didn't notice the steep, winding roads, the deeper, greener, lusher vegetation, nor the pale, misty foothills receding layer upon layer into the distance.

He didn't notice the different faces; paler, more mongoloid with rosy cheeks and eyes wrinkled with wind and laughter and bodies wiry from climbing.

They crossed a rickety, wooden bridge which led them over a lime green, burbling river to a bank on the other side where stood a small, grey, stone Hindu temple.

Its mirror image reflected in the ripples of the river at the edge of a narrow promontory; its oblong dome rose with quiet dignity upwards from a quadrangular base. Round about were scattered antique stones, ruined porticos and broken statues, yet all somehow managing to seem part of the overall design.

But Ronnie was not able to appreciate any of it. He stumbled down the steps which led from the temple to the water's edge, and sprawled, half in, half out, lapping like an exhausted animal.

'What am I going to do?' he whispered. 'I don't know where I am or where I'm going. I've reached the mountains but look at them!' He stretched an arm and feebly took in a whole panorama of hills with his gesture. 'A hundred years wouldn't be enough time to find anyone in there.' He dropped his head on his arm.

The keeper of the temple stood in the square, intricately carved wooden doorway. Deepak saw him and approached reverentially with bowed head. 'Maharaj-ji, I have brought a friend to you. He is fainting with hunger and weariness. Can he rest here for a while? I will get food for him.'

The keeper walked down the steps and stood where his shadow fell over the distraught boy. 'Ah! Those from the West are not used to going for long on an empty stomach, eh?' He grinned mischievously and touched his shoulder. 'Come! Come, young man, out of the sun and rest in the shade of the verandah.'

Ronnie smiled despite himself. 'So I still look a Westerner! Like a British Indian?'

Deepak mocked him. 'You look a pukkah Indian now, Ronnie.' He looked at Ronnie's long, thin body and his cotton trousers clinging wet to his legs, and his grubby T-shirt hanging loose. 'But Maharah-ji sees everything. There are no secrets from him.'

Ronnie looked up at the keeper and wondered what Deepak meant.

He looked more like a clown than a holy man. He was round and fat and bubbly, and his whole frame wobbled and shook when he laughed; indeed, he seemed to be in a state of perpetual laughter. His face was bursting with a mysterious humour which twitched at his lips and danced in his black, glittering eyes.

Ronnie sighed wearily. He wasn't in the mood for jokes. He managed to thank him politely for permission to rest on his verandah, and avoiding further eye contact, climbed the steps into the shade.

'Stay, Ronnie. Rest well. I'll be back soon!' cried Deepak. 'And we'll feast like kings!'

Ronnie, watching him go, felt a pang of fear. He had come to rely on Deepak. 'Come back, won't you,' he called after him. 'For God's sake, come back,' he cried to himself.

'The boy will return, don't worry,' the keeper reassured him. 'Meanwhile won't you partake of this coconut with me? It will stave off your hunger for a while. You have a bowl in your rucksack. Bring it out, please, and I will pour the milk from the coconut into it.'

Ronnie looked blankly at his rucksack. How could the keeper tell that he had a bowl in it? There was no bulge, no protruding shape which gave it away. Puzzled, but obedient, Ronnie took out the bowl and placed it on the verandah between them. All the time, he watched the keeper, wondering if he too would recoil, or see something significant in it, as the holy man had done in Durgapur. But his host just nodded and smiled genially, murmuring, 'Good, good, good.' He took a sharp stone and struck the coconut on its softest point at the top. Then he tipped it over the bowl and a long, thin white liquid poured into it.

Only when the keeper took up the bowl into both his cupped hands, did Ronnie detect a slight quiver running through his body, a momentary closing of the eyes like a slow blink, before handing it to Ronnie.

'I like the shape of your bowl,' he said softly. 'It is as perfect as the sound, "Ôm".'

Ronnie took it abruptly. 'Yes,' he said bluntly. 'My father gave it to me.'

'One day, there will be no father, no mother, no son. One day you will only see this object, and only hear the one sound, "Óm".'

'God, he's a right crackpot,' Ronnie thought to himself, then immediately regretted his thought. Looking into the keeper's eyes, he knew that the keeper knew what had just gone through his mind. He felt the blood of embarrassment flood into his face.

'Go on, drink!' urged the keeper.

Ronnie drank, and ate the pieces of coconut which the man shelled and broke off for him. Then as if to reconcile himself with the keeper, he said, 'Thank you for your kindness. I feel much better now. Thank you.'

The keeper giggled as if Ronnie had cracked a joke. 'No, no, no! No thanks. It is Dharma. It is my duty. Now rest. I must see to the temple.' He got up from his haunches, and moving with extraordinary grace for a man of his weight, glided to the doorway. Before going inside, he suddenly stopped. The suppressed giggle still puckered his cheeks. 'Oh, and young man!' he chortled. 'Deepak's dream will lead you to your friend. Won't that be wonderful, old chap? Then you can continue your search together.'

'Won't that be wonderful, old chap . . . old chap . . . old chap . . .' There was a quaint English public-school manner in the way he had used that expression. Ronnie leapt to his feet and rushed after him into the darkness of the temple. The keeper's face glowed in the flickering flames of the holy fire which burned there beneath the shrine of the god Shiva and his wife Parvati. Ronnie gripped his arm. 'You . . . you?' He stared desperately in the man's face, looking for recognition.

'Are you . . . ?'

'No, my son, I am not your father.' His face became utterly still, as if he had been turned to stone like the gods around him.

171

When he spoke again his voice was high, almost breathless. 'I teased you, a moment ago. Forgive me. It was to wake you up. To give you hope. If you give in to despair, you will lose sight of your goal and you will never find what you are searching for. Go now. Clear your head of troubles. The forces of your mind are scattered. Concentrate on the bowl. Concentrate on its beauty of shape and simplicity of use. Concentrate, Ronnie, and become one with the object. Then all will be dissolved into Self and the road to the future will become clear.'

Midday burned into a white heat. Ronnie stared at the river through half-shut eyes. It glittered almost black, drained of colour by the sun's brightness. The silhouette of a man waded into the water. The clarity of his outline showed that he was naked to the waist and his dhoti clung to his legs, emphasising his gaunt, bony body. He stooped with cupped hands, filled them with water then raised them above his head with outstretched arms. Then he allowed the water to trickle down on to his head. He stooped again and again, each time cupping his hands with water. Each time, he washed his face, his forearms, his hands and his feet, and finally submerged his whole body into the water. When he emerged from the water, it was as if his body was on fire, for every drop of water, glistening on his skin, caught the sunlight and set him ablaze.

Ronnie's eyes moved back to the bowl It was hard to concentrate. Five or ten seconds, and his eye would move to something else, or his mind would wander from its concentration on the bowl again. He sat cross-legged, trying to breathe rhythmically, remembering the holy man he had watched in Delhi; how he had breathed in, long and slow, and then with his expelled breath made the sound of 'Ôm'.

'How does he know?' The question jangled round his brain. The keeper could see things that were unseen; read thoughts that were unspoken. How could he know he was searching for his father? How could he know about Deepak's dream?

Ronnie breathed in and closed his eyes. 'Ôm.' He breathed out slowly. He breathed in. The question was asked again and again. He breathed out. 'Ôm.' A pinprick of light burned between his eyes. Ronnie focused on it inwardly. How . . . does he . . . know . . . He breathed in. The colour blue flooded through his mind as if he had breathed in the ocean. 'Ôm.' He breathed out. How does . . . the blue grew deeper. The question was obliterated. Beautiful shapes descended through the blue, forming and re-forming; colours and sounds harmonised with each other, making music. The music grew louder and louder, filling him with such a sweetness that all thought was banished from his brain. He breathed in. He forgot his hunger, his tiredness, his anxieties, even his search. There was only the very first beginnings, the palest glimmering of . . . Self.

'Ronnie!'

Ronnie breathed out slowly and opened his eyes. 'How long have I been sitting here?'

'A long time.'

'Must we go now?'

'Soon. When we have eaten.'

Ronnie got slowly to his feet and stretched. He expected to feel stiff and dizzy, but his limbs unwound as if they had been oiled, and his brain felt light and clear.

'They speak of a Westerner in the town. A hippy.'

'Oh?' At last Ronnie looked at Deepak who was standing shyly a little way off.

'We must speak to a child called Shanta and her brother Amar. They know something.'

'Are you afraid, Deepak?' asked Ronnie.

Deepak didn't answer. He moved towards him and put down a cloth bundle on the verandah between them. 'Come, eat,' he said, spreading it out, and revealing paper packages of pooris and vegetables. 'Then we'll go.'

Ronnie felt quite calm as he followed Deepak along the railway track into the sidings. He knew they would find Ed before the day was out.

All around them was a scurrying and a murmuring. All around was a whispering and giggling, a shuffling and muttering. Suddenly, in the bleak landscape of railway sheds, broken-down engines, disused carriages, of slag heaps and chippings, banks and ditches, they had entered a kingdom of children. They seemed to converge on them from everywhere: hard, little bodies, hard-as-nails bodies, grey with ash; flat, cracked bare feet, grasping bony fingers, elbows, knees, sticking-out joints, matchstick legs and pot bellies, hair bleached orange by the sun and lack of vitamins, and their eyes: eyes which watched, eyes which followed, eyes darting with wariness, bubbling with laughter, running with infections, weeping with despair; eyes which examined, judged, assessed and waited. These were the destitutes; the children, who like Deepak, rode the trains up and down the country, clawing out a survival, scraping, eating and sleeping rough. These were the runaways; the children whose parents were dead or too poor to keep them; or like Deepak, they were kidnapped children, escaping from tyranny and exploitation, on the run, living by their wits, charm, intelligence and cunning.

They greeted Deepak with shrill cries, forming a nudging, jostling, good-natured entourage, as they made their way along the track.

Deepak stopped before a long piece of rusty corrugated-iron propped up against the side of a ditch. From it were draped bits and pieces of fluttering rags held in place by stones. Deepak called out, 'Amar! Eh, Amar!'

A long bony arm and then a leg and then an emaciated body prised itself through the rags and iron. Amar stood before them, solemnly.

Deepak spoke rapidly. He looked at Ronnie and gesticulated and smiled as if to reassure him. Amar would not smile, but he did nod an agreement that they should enter his dwelling, so as all the children crowded chattering and inquisitive around the entrance, Deepak and Ronnie crawled inside.

Rows of silver shoes. Tiny, sparkling, silver shoes, small enough for two pairs to fit on the palm of one hand. They glinted like little jewels, amazingly beautiful, as if they had dropped out of the sky and landed by chance in this hovel, this remnant of hell on earth.

Yet when Ronnie looked closer, they were not diamonds or pearls or even the glass Cinderella's slippers had been made from, they were made from rubbish; from litter, scrap heaps, rubbish dumps; sweet papers, silver foil, cardboard and tissue paper. Only a child's mind would have thought of it, only a child's eye would have gathered the materials and only a child's fingers could have fashioned these miniature, fairy shoes and placed them in rows for the whole world to admire.

'She makes them and sells them,' said Deepak.

The manufacturer of the shoes lay invisibly buried beneath a covering of rags.

'Shanta!' Amar bent down and gently pulled some of the rags away. He revealed a little girl of not more than six years old?

'She is ill,' whispered Deepak. 'Amar is very worried. But it is Shanta who can tell us something about this Westerner.'

The child groaned pitifully and opened her eyes. They were bright with fever. Amar and Deepak both questioned her:

'Did you sell shoes to a Westerner?'

'Yes. He gave me five rupees! Five whole rupees!' she gave a weak but triumphant smile.

'Enough to feed us for days!' exclaimed Amar proudly.

'When did you sell them to him?'

'Three days ago. He was kind. He only took one pair even though he paid so much.'

'Then where did he go?'

'He was ill. He held his stomach in pain. He asked where he could find a room. I told him Sanjay, the sweet-seller, had a room above his shop. He could try. I led him there. I had to hold his arm sometimes, he was staggering and nearly fainting. Sanjay didn't want him. Tried to send him away. I told him God would be angered. Anyway, the Westerner gave him lots of money, so Sanjay agreed. It's a stinking room. This place is better.' She tossed her head defiantly.

'Is he still there?'

'Yes,' Amar answered that one. 'He hasn't left the room for three days.'

Deepak translated everything for Ronnie. 'He's still there.'

It was a strange moment to think of Grandpa, of Henry Saville. Suddenly, Ronnie almost felt that the old man was kneeling beside him.

'Did you know about this kind of India, Grandpa?' he asked.

'How could I, Ronnie? We were protected from all that.'

'What, Ronnie?' Deepak was puzzled.

'I was only wondering out loud,' murmured Ronnie. 'Wondering whether my English grandfather knew where my search would take me.'

'Shall we go?' Deepak crouched down before the doorway, ready to leave.

'Who will look after her?' asked Ronnie, looking at the little girl lying like a wounded bird on her bed of rags.

Deepak shrugged. 'God, I suppose.'

For a while they were followed. Everyone was willing to be their guide, but as they reached the bazaar and plunged into the warren of little streets Deepak grew quieter as he became more and more sure of his route.

A strong sweet smell of bubbling sugar and boiled milk drifted down the street towards them. Silent now, the two boys walked on until inevitably, they stood before Sanjay's Sweet Shop.

Sanjay himself, a vast bulk of fat and flesh who looked as if he, too, were made entirely of milk and sugar like his sweets, stirred huge cauldrons of syrup and fat. Ronnie thought of the thin, wretched children scavenging for food round the railway tracks and felt an unreasonable surge of anger, but Sanjay didn't even look up. When Deepak spoke to him he just waved an indifferent hand, indicating that they should go round to the back of the filthy, crumbling, dilapidated building.

Ronnie knew that they stood in Deepak's dream. This was how it was. His heart thumped. They pushed open the ancient door and stared up the dark, foul-smelling staircase. They hesitated, listened. All was silent. Suddenly, Deepak retreated as fast as a rabbit and flung himself round the corner. Ronnie sprang after him and caught his arm. 'Hey! Deepak! There's nothing to be scared of. If it's Ed, he's OK. He may be sick, but he's OK.'

Deepak hung his head, shaking it fearfully. 'There is evil. I can smell it. I can feel it, here, here and here,' he struck his head, heart and stomach. 'There are bad spirits. I'm sure of it. We mustn't go up.'

'I have to.' Ronnie let go Deepak's arm. They boy was shaking. He patted him gently. 'Wait here, then. You don't have to come in. I'll go, but wait for me, won't you?'

Deepak nodded vigorously without looking up, and Ronnie went rapidly back to the doorway. He could feel his resolve weakening, and Deepak's fear infecting him, too. He put a foot on the first tread of the stair, then another, then another. He reached the top. The smell was terrible, but it was not just a smell of a dilapidated building, of unformed sewers, open drains and bubbling sugar. There was a smell of something unimaginably evil. It seeped out of the mouldering walls, yet it wasn't the walls; it lurked secretly down the rotting stairway, yet it wasn't the stairs. Ronnie couldn't define it, he couldn't say why. All he knew was that he was filled with an overpowering impulse to run away as Deepak had done. He clutched his rucksack to feel the reassurance of the bowl. He took one step forwards, then one step back and was about to turn and flee the building when a voice called out:

'Hey, Ronnie! That you? Geeze, you took your time. I've been waiting for you.'

22
THE STRUGGLE

The door was half open to the room at the top of the stairs. From where he stood he could see only emptiness and gloom, and a feeble shaft of light emanating from some unseen grating to the outside world, which fell, struggling with dust particles, like a sinister spotlight.

He stepped into the threshold. The dimensions of the room were blurred by the dusty darkness. He could hardly distinguish floor from ceiling or wall from wall.

Gradually his eyes adjusted and the room came slowly into focus. It was then that he saw the stolen bowl placed, as if ceremoniously, in the middle of the room on the floor.

Ronnie took two rapid steps towards it; would have scooped it up and fled, but a voice rasped out, 'Don't touch it!'

Ed! He would have missed him in the gloom but for a flash of eyes and a white face turning.

'What kept you?' Ed sneered. 'Don't touch that . . . don't . . !' His voice rose to a scream.

Too late, Ronnie grabbed at the bowl. It was like touching high-voltage electricity. Something hurled him bodily across the room.

'I told you to leave it!'

Ronnie moaned and clutched his rucksack to him as if for protection. The room was filled with whispering.

'I took your bowl, but I wasn't really stealing it. I needed it. It was my last chance. You see, I recognised the kind of bowl it was. I'd seen some like them before, in Nepal in the temples. Meditation bowls. More than that – they communicate with spirits; but there's good and bad . . . good and bad . . . I had to take the risk. You see, I got to get off these drugs or, I'm a goner . . . Do you see? That's why I took the bowl. 'Sides, I reckoned I was doing you a favour. I knew you'd follow me. You had to. It got you away from that shit Mike. You'll see, I did you a favour. Got you out on the road. I was waiting for you. See? You found me, didn't you. We've both got a chance now . . . if . . .'

'If what?' Ronnie crawled across the room towards him, his body aching with the blow. 'If you can get hold of your next fix, you mean!' Ronnie's voice was bitter with sarcasm.

'No, no!' Ed thumped the floor in front of him with his fist. 'Not any more. I've hit the bottom now. My last fix was a dupe. I was cheated. It made me ill. Could have killed me. I had no choice but to try and go cold turkey – sweat it out. Alone. I thought the bowl would help me. I played it and played it, trying to keep my mind off the pain, the cramps, the hallucinations. I must have played that bowl for nearly three days and nights . . . but something happened. I played it too hard, too long . . . I couldn't stop . . . even when I knew . . ! Oh God!' His voice broke into harsh sobs.

'Knew what?' yelled Ronnie. 'What did you know?

'I got the feeling there was something bad. Evil. A demonic spirit trapped inside the bowl. They believe these things, you know.' His voice suddenly dropped till it was practically inaudible. 'I let it out, Ronnie. It's in here. It won't let us go. We're doomed, you know, unless . . .' He crawled over to him and whispered in his ear, 'Unless you got your bowl. You try playing yours . . .' He grabbed at the rucksack on Ronnie's back and tried to wrench it from him.

Ronnie pushed him away angrily. 'You bloody idiot. Your brain's gone soft. That's what drugs do to you. I'm going to get a doctor, or help.' He tried to get to his feet and lunged for the door, but suddenly, it was as if his feet had become rooted to the floor. He fell face down with a cry of despair. .

'Didn't I tell you? Didn't I tell you? Oh God, what have I done? Play the bowl, play the bowl!' The whispering around him increased, echoing and reverberating, cavernous, subterranean.

Ronnie's arms clasped his rucksack to him. Panic surged up his throat. He tried again to get up, but couldn't. He looked for Ed. He was crouched in a corner, but he looked different. The whispering became sharper, more like hissing. It no longer sounded human. Ed crouched, but he was changing, and his crouching was like a wild animal's. He was drawing himself into a tight, flexed piece of energy, ready for attack. His eyes gleamed; his teeth bared. They stared at each other.

'Death.' Ronnie ripped open his rucksack. The bowl. He had to get the bowl, or death would take him.

He had only just got it between his hands and knees as he crouched on the floor, when Ed sprang; was it Ed? Or was it some wild animal? It flew through the air and landed on his back. He sprawled across the bowl, winded. He felt burning breath and teeth and claws tearing at his back and head.

The two bodies rolled, locked together in a desperate frenzy, and yet, somehow, Ronnie kept hold of the bowl. He struggled and fought and then with the bowl clasped in both hands like a weapon, he struck out.

'Ôm.' He felt the creature's hold loosen. Ronnie curled himself up into a ball around the bowl, and pressed his lips to the rim. 'Ôm.' There was no up or down as the room began to spin. He was caught in a whirlpool, a maelstrom of howling and screaming. 'Ôm.' He felt his lungs bursting for air, the blood rushing into his eyes and nose. He was dying. Death was getting him after all.

Somewhere in the far, far distance, he heard a high-pitched cry. 'Ron-ee!' '*Ôm.*' The sound was like a tolling bell. He didn't know how long it had been sounding. Possibly for ever. '*Ôm . . . Ôm . . . Ôm*' In his mind he was running down the stairs out into the street. 'Deepak?' The boy had gone. 'Deepak! You said you'd wait. Come back!'

Floating, as in a dream, he made his way down the empty street towards the market place. Deepak stood on the roadside looking across to the flower market. He turned to Ronnie with brimming eyes. 'My mother is there! Look, do you see her?'

A woman in a white saree, her arms filled with long-stemmed flowers smiled and waved. 'Come!' she cried.

'*Ôm.*' There was a smell of tube lilies and sugar and syrup. The screaming got louder. '*Ôm.*' Deepak was running towards the woman. Already she was beginning to fade. 'Mother! Mother! Is it you?' The huge, brightly painted truck came hurtling round the corner with silver goddesses bobbing in the windscreen.

'*Ôm.*' He couldn't breathe. Couldn't shout a warning. The voices of the crowd that gathered rose and fell like the sounds of the sea.

'The boy just ran out. The driver didn't have a chance to stop. He can't be blamed.'

'*Ôm.*' Ronnie wondered if he, too, was dying. He had no more breath even to cry. Darkness swirled around him. Yet if he was also dead, his soul was free, flying on a trapeze, swooping across oceans and continents. He thought death had made him blind and deaf, yet he could see and hear such a parade of images and sounds.

Sounds and smells of an Indian forest. Soft singing and woodburning. An old holy man murmured, 'Ram Ram!' and stoked the fire, a young woman rocked and sang to her baby. The baby turned its head and looked straight into his eyes. The eyes grew and grew like shining oceans, reflecting all of the past and present within them. There was Henry Saville, he smiled and waved, and his young wife Isabella clung happily to his arm. There was the baby. A baby within a baby. A brown baby held between white arms. The baby became a boy, and then the boy became a man.

It was his father, Ronnie knew it, and there was Linda, his mother. How young she looked. Now she had a baby. She held it out to his father as if presenting him with a gift. His father took the baby. It was he. Ronnie. He was the baby. His father kissed him, hugged him, rocked him and held him. His flesh. His blood. They would always belong, no matter what. He cried out. 'Father!'

The faces sharpened, dimmed, faded and disappeared.

'Ôm.' Ronnie breathed in. 'Ôm.' He breathed out long and slow.

There was silence now. Ronnie looked up. 'He did love me.' The grey shaft of light had almost gone. The stolen bowl still stood in the centre of the room. Spread-eagled, on the floor, as one who had been thrown from a great height, lay Ed.

Ronnie crawled over to him and laid his head over his heart. He could hear it beating, faint but regular. He slept.

They awoke before dawn. They gathered up the bowls and set off towards the temple. As they crossed the bridge, a thin, long crack of daylight opened up in the night sky. Down on the shore, flimsy figures of children wandered about collecting wood.

Ronnie and Ed entered the temple. Within its windowless heart, the single flame from the sacred fire threw shadows over the faces of the gods, Shiva and Paravati; it cast a glow over the face of the keeper, sitting cross-legged, his eyes closed, still as a statue.

Deepak's body lay before them on a mat. His body had been strewn with flowers to hide the wounds, and his hands clasped long-stemmed lilies.

'Maharaj-ji!'

The keeper opened his eyes, looked at the two young men. He smiled a smile to calm them, then closed them again with a sigh.

When the children had built the funeral pyre, the burning rim of the sun had just burst upon the horizon. They came and told the keeper.

It was the best funeral pyre. Made from the ordinary brittle fragments of driftwood and branches which the children had collected from the river bank. The keeper came down with sandalwood and a jar of clarified butter. This pyre would be fit for a Brahman.

Ed and Ronnie carried Deepak's body on its matting down from the temple and gently laid it in the heart of the pyre. The keeper placed the sandalwood around him and dashed on the clarified butter as he uttered prayers to God. Finally he lit one brand and when it was aflame, he walked all round the pyre, setting it alight.

There was the crack of contact, and flames shot into the air.

Somewhere in his head, Ronnie could hear the notes of the singing bowls spiralling up into the sky like larks.

They said his spirit rose with the smoke and flames. They cast his ashes into the river, and said that because the river flowed into the Mother Ganges, his soul would be assured of eternal peace.

'It was all my fault.' Ed knelt in the darkness of the temple.

'Are you so arrogant,' asked the keeper, 'to think that you can take the responsibility for something which was decreed by God? If you were to blame, then why not Ronnie, who brought the bowls to India? Or Henry Saville, for giving them to him. Or his father for leaving them, or for the wife who did not cast herself on her husband's funeral pyre? How far back must we go to pin the blame?

'No. We each have our own paths to follow. You grieve for him who should not be grieved for. If you are wise, you never grieve, neither for the living nor the dead. There was never a time when Deepak did not exist, nor will there be a future in which he does not exist. A Soul does not die when a body is slain. Fire cannot burn him, nor water wet him, nor the wind

184

dry him. Just remember, he is always being born and always dying. If you understand that, then you will never grieve.'

But Ronnie did grieve.

One day; three days had passed by, or was it four or five? Time ceased to mean much to Ronnie: the only measurement that counted was when the pain began to ease, and when he learnt that finding Self meant that he could forget about himself. But one day Ed came and sat beside him on the temple steps. Together they stared at the reflection of the temple quivering in the quiet ripples of the river.

'It is time to go now,' he said. 'Meet your father.'

Ronnie knew he was right. The time was right. He was ready now.

They had both changed. Ed had changed. The hunted look had gone from his face and been replaced by a serenity, even wisdom.

'Did you find what you were looking for?' asked Ronnie.

'Yes, I did. If only I'd trusted, perhaps I would have found my way more quickly. We fight and struggle; look for shortcuts and short remedies, when all the time we carry the secrets of Heaven and Hell inside ourselves.'

'You're beginning to sound like the Maharaj-ji.' Ronnie smiled. It was the first smile since Deepak died.

They packed up their rucksacks and the singing bowls and set off towards the everlasting snows. Sometimes they walked, sometimes they rode with horse traders who were returning to their mountain kingdoms. It was the busy pilgrim trail and they never needed to ask the way. They didn't know where they were going, but they knew they would know when they got there.

At last, one day, when they had left the soft, warm valleys, climbed above the perilous slopes of pine and deodar trees, when they had crossed fierce mountain rivers and moved on to the hard, glacial rock of the mountains themselves, they reached a small temple built into the rock.

They would not have noticed it but for the ragged orange flag fluttering on the end of a long bamboo pole.

Inside the darkness of the grey phallic-shaped dome, an old, old priest sat before the sacred flame chanting prayers. He neither glanced up nor halted, even for a second, when the two travellers entered through the low, square, stone doorway.

Ronnie and Ed stood barefooted, quiet and respectful, absorbing the deep sense of peace. As their eyes adjusted to the gloom, they realised that one whole wall of the rock was hewn out into an image of Vishnu, The Preserver. He was a massive figure with four arms, sitting on a coiled serpent with his wife, the Goddess, Lakshmi, at his side. Their eyes travelled over the calm, serene features, marvelling at the tenderness and wisdom that breathed out of the ancient stone.

At the base of the relief were small clusters of offerings left by pilgrims; garlands of flowers, handfuls of rice, piles of sweetmeats and dishes of food.

A little to one side, half in shadow, stood a single, metal bowl. Its rim was wide, though its neck was slender as a chalice. The sacred flame flickered orange in its reflecting body. Ronnie knelt before it and touched the rim with his finger. He felt the tremor of a single note.

His journey was at an end. Ronnie knew he had arrived.

He took out the two singing bowls and placed them with the other at the foot of the god. He stood for a long while, till his excitement had calmed down and his brain was clear, then with a long, deep breath he murmured, 'I am ready,' and stepped outside.

On a snowy peak, piercing the blue sky, a little way above the temple, a solitary figure stood watching and waiting.

Ronnie began to walk towards him.

EPILOGUE

6 JANUARY 1989
14, LYNTON GROVE,
LONDON W4

Dear Ed,

It was great to get your letter at last.

I knew you would return to India. When I received no answer to the letter I sent to San Francisco, I knew you must have gone back to the Maharaj-ji at the temple. It is the only thing that consoles me about Deepak's death. The only thing that can justify it, is the knowledge that he was a part of me finding my father and you finding your spiritual teacher.

Sometimes I feel I've never left the river temple. I wonder if you ever glimpse me walking along the shore, or sitting on the temple steps? I don't think a single day goes by when I do not think of India. Never a day goes by when I do not remember our friendship and companionship.

I never told you about my meeting with my father. At the end you just waited patiently for me at the foot of the mountain, and when I returned you asked no questions. I just went back to Durgapur and hardly even said "goodbye".

The meeting with my father was both momentous and insignificant. We met face to face; hugged, touched, looked at each other and recognised each other for what we were, father and son. That was momentous. But then we both realised we had gone beyond that. It was something, but nothing. It was as pre-ordained as Halley's Comet circumventing our galaxy and passing our planet

Earth at a precisely calculated moment, but leaving as little impact.

Our meeting was more an acknowledgement; that we were as bound to each other by flesh and blood as the stars and planets are bound to their universe, but there could be no more than that. We each have our own path to follow. The words were true. It is only for the sake of Self that the son is dear. Only for the sake of Self that the father is dear. He has found himself now, and I am close to finding myself. It is enough.

As for my mother, I think she had always loved my father, though I thought she hated him. Deep down, under all the hurt and anger, she never really stopped loving him. It would have been easier if he had died. India was important for her, too. She came to see that though he wasn't dead, neither was he alive for her. I was able to tell her that, and it has helped to finally close that part of her life once and for all. There is reconciliation.

But you'll be glad to know that Mike and my mum split up after they got back. He was wrong for her. I knew that. So did you, just from looking at him. Trouble is, she was lonely and he really loved her, as far as such a bone-headed guy is able to love in between loving himself. India taught her something, too, even though she was ill most of the time. Just think, if she hadn't gone to India she might have married Mike, and then she would never have met this smashing guy called Steve. He's a painter, and even I like him! I think it's for real. Taken ten years off my mum. She looks like a teenager!

You told me you got back to the States to find your wife had left you and gone with your daughter to live in New York. You seem to accept it very philosophically. As the Maharaj-ji would have said, "It was pre-ordained". He loves you, you know. You were searching for the true teacher. He was searching for the true pupil and found you. He told me you had the "gift" and said you would become a great teacher, too. He said you had the power to discover the "Kundalini" – I hope you are now feeling at peace with yourself.

I wish you could have met my grandfather, Henry Saville. Isn't it strange how the threads of his life, even after he died, came to be bound up in the threads of your life? Somehow, he was the hub of the wheel around which both out lives revolved for a while. He loved India. I do too now. I will return one day, though not yet.

Until I went to India, I had no idea what I wanted to do with my life. I had no particular talent. I wasn't amazingly good at anything. It was only when I got back to England that I realised I had returned with a purpose. I shall finish school and try and go into Medicine. Then I'll go back.

You talk about setting up an ashram to help destitute children like Deepak. One day, Ed, I'll come and join you, when I'm a doctor and can be of real use.

Till then, stay in touch. Write often.

Yours ever,

Ronnie.

GERALDINE KAYE

A Breath of Fresh Air

Amy Smith lives in Bristol with her Grandmother as her mother is often away from home, pursuing her career as a singer. Amy has never known her father, only that some mystery surrounds him. However, at school she is increasingly absorbed by a class project, 'Bristol and the Slavery Connection' and becomes obsessed by images of the past which haunt her imagination. One night, during a thunder storm, Amy glimpses a slave girl outside her window, and the past takes over.

'Geraldine Kaye recreates the horrors of the slave trade with enormous sensitivity and also with a clear eye for historical accuracy. The result is a book which both informs and moves.'
    Children's Books of the Year 1988

ANTHONY MASTERS

All the Fun of the Fair

Jim North and his Gallopers – a beautifully painted and carved fairground ride – have an annual date at the Starling Point estate. But this year they have not bargained for the dramatic end of Gerry Kitson's mystery ride, nor the arrival of their new assistant, Leroy. And as Leroy desperately tries to prove himself, the battle to save the Gallopers, not only from bankruptcy but also from vandalism, begins.

ALL THE FUN OF THE FAIR is the first in the *Starling Point* series. Other titles available are:

Cat Burglars
Siege
African Queen